Water Shows the Hidden Heart

Valley-dwellers

This edition first published in 2005 by
Valley-dwellers

website: www.valley-dwellers.com
e-mail: info@valley-dwellers.com

10 9 8 7 6 5 4 3 2 1

This edition © Roma Ryan 2005
Roma Ryan is hereby identified as author of this work
Photography copyright Persia Ryan 2005
All rights reserved.

No part of this publication may be reproduced, stored in a retrieval system, transmitted in any form or any means, electronic, mechanical, photocopying, recording or otherwise, without the prior permission of the publisher.

This book is sold subject to the condition that is shall not, by way of trade or otherwise, be lent, re-sold, hired out or otherwise circulated without the publisher's prior consent in any form of binding or cover other than that in which it is published and without a similar condition including this condition being imposed on the subsequent purchaser.

A CIP record for this book is available from the British Library.

ISBN 0-9552011-0-1

Lyrics reproduced by kind permission of EMI Music Publishing Ltd
'Amarantine' album cover courtesy Warner Music

Editor: Ebony Ryan
Front cover photography: Persia Ryan
Photograph of Enya: Simon Fowler
Jacket Design by Origin Design
Typeset by Origin Design
Printed and bound by MPG Books Ltd

for
Ernest

for
Eleanor

Part one:

The Songs of the Loxians

ᐯᔕᐳᑎᑎᗯᛁ₹₹ᐸᐱ ᐱ ᐳᐱ
Water shows the hidden heart

Let me tell you…
Everywhere
The City of Constellations
Nothing is ever lost
The City of Constellations
The Islands the rain made
The East Wall
They do not know why
The Song of the Loxians
The lost words of the Valley-dwellers
The first words
The fragments
…of words that exist…
one of those, looking…

Part two:

Water shows the hidden heart

The Wanderer
The Place of Rains
The City of Indecision and Doubt
The Island of the house-the-colour-of-the-sea
The Plain of Mementoes
The Valley of lost time

The City of End and Endlessness
The Isle of Revenants
The City of Solitudes
The City of the Distance from you
The City of Words of blue and yellow and green and red
The City of Sleep
Where the scent of love lies, sleeping
The Cities that do not Exist, exist
The City of Realisations
Mount Orison
The City of Days
The Tree of the Lost
North of his love
A road through a valley in darkness
The Islands that are not of this world
A City of Silver
The way of the eremite
The Valley where the moon is caught in the trees
Water shows the hidden heart
Endlong into midnight
The Parable of Day
The Room of Books
Amarantine
The Room of Books

The written breath of the other:
Translations of the songs of the Loxians

Foreword

Enya is three people - Roma, Nicky and myself. We have worked together since the beginning, and the road through our musical history has been an exciting and fulfilling journey for us all. It has been filled with magic, and part of that magic are the words Roma writes for us.

When we embarked on "*Amarantine*" our sixth album, in September 2003, I had no idea I would be singing not only in Japanese but in a language created by Roma, which she calls *Loxian*.

In order to give both substance and reason to the language, Roma created her own world for the "*Loxians*". This world is contained within these pages and it was from this story that three of the songs on "*Amarantine*" took shape.

I have always loved Roma's lyrics, I cannot imagine my music without her words. She writes my voice. I sing her heart. Nicky makes everything possible.

I love this story. Although it may seem to belong to the world of the fabulist, for me it also combines a sense of reality with the emotional. It brings us closer to the way Roma thinks as lyricist, poet and storyteller.

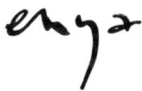

Part One

The Songs of the Loxians

From the City of Constellations

to the wanderer
and a Place of Rains
he journeys on…

…the City of Hesitation and Doubt
the Island of the house-the-colour-of-the-sea
the Plain of Mementoes
he journeys on to find his love…

…the Valley of lost time
the City of End and Endlessness
the Isle of Revenants
he journeys on…

…the City of Solitudes
the City of the Distance from you
the City of Words of blue and yellow and red and green
he journeys onto find his love…

…where the road takes him through
the City of Sleep
the thinking that does not end is within him.
Then he dreams
the scent of love lies, sleeping.
The road takes him,
this man who is searching,
it brings him
in silence through the night,
to where the Cities that do not Exist, exist.

It brings him
in silence through the night
close to the City of Realisations;
it is here one finds the way...

...Mount Orison
the City of Days
the Tree of the Lost
he journeys on...

...north of his love
a road through a valley in darkness
the Islands that are not of this world
a City of Silver,
he journeys on to find his love...

It is a long way through darkness
to the way of the eremite
the eremite sings of the world and of
the journey of love, which is not lost in eternity

...the Valley where the moon is caught in the trees
water shows the hidden heart
endlong into midnight
he journeys on...

...the parable of day
the Room of Books
where the winds come to him and say....

Let Me Tell You

They say these words are but the first words in a book of words. They say they are an atlas for those who are looking for those who are lost. They say these words are but the first words in a book that holds many other writings. They say these writings are of the night, and that they are words of love, page upon page bound in black, a black that is the colour of the night, the night whose heart does not stop beating.

The pages are torn, the script has come from long ago, it is indigo written in the hands of autumn, of winter, of the other seasons. These writings of the night are wrapped in ebony. One expects to find some tracery of stars upon its cover, some part of the night announcing itself, but there is no map, no portolan, no constellation. It holds upon its shoulders these words: The Black Book of the Night.

They say these words were uttered in the night. They say these words are the words of a man searching, a man with sadness in his heart, a man looking for a love he has lost and cannot find. They say these words are his immrama, his purrhayso, his odyssey.* They say every word scattered on these pages comes from his heart.

They say there are other books of the night that hold other words, that hold more of the story of his love. It has been heard tell of the Red Book of the Night, the Indigo, the Silver. But they have not yet been found, although always there are those who are looking for that which is lost. They are a mystery, as are the books of prophecy, the books whose prophecies cannot be told. They are the Five Books of Prophecy, but one had been destroyed by water, one burnt by fire, one buried in the earth, one has disappeared into the air and one will only be known in time.

They say the Black Book of the Night is held in the City of Constellations. But there are two cities which bear this name, so there are two books which bear the same name. The only words that do not differ, that are exact down to the last comma, are these first words in a book of words. They say all other words written onto their pages come from the same source, from the one who is looking for whom he loves, but each city has given to the Black Book of the Night its own translation.

Each city claims to have the original, to be the true bearer of the words of night.

Let me tell you of these cities:

The City of Constellations:

Everything lies somewhere in the night:

the sound of the sea making its way to the shore,
the grief a man speaks,
the spectacle of sun as it lays itself down on the hillside, sleeping,
the moon and her weeping; her heart breaking
into a million silver pieces.

The sorrow a man shoulders,
the rib's ridge, the curve of a road.
The carillon of hours and days and years.
The words a man fears.
Clothes, unrobed.

The miles a man cannot find.
Those places nobody truly knows.
The sound of the island in the winds.
Freedom and repose.

Starlight. Moonlight. Sunlight.
The afterglow of embers.
The fall of each hidden city a man dreams of.
All a man remembers.

Nothing is ever lost.
This is what is told in the heights:
everything lies somewhere in the night...

The Heights

The City of Constellations, the city of the stillness of nightshapes, the one that breathes in the heights of the mountain, the one that sits on the edge as if alone in the night, that knows of the valley but seldom goes there, is alive in darkness. Within the walls of this city are the Astronomers, the Star Keepers, the Sentries - the Loxians. They are those who stand in the heights of the Heights and watch the night, they are those who listen. They listen for the voice of the stars, listen for others who may be as themselves; watching, listening, speaking, waiting. They are like warriors armed with ink and paper, with symbols, with scripts, with glass and mirror and calculation. Their bows are numerals, their arrows are words they send out into where they cannot see. They do not know how far their words will travel, or for how long they will cry out in the endlessness, or if they will ever reach anywhere. But the Loxians keep faith. They persevere. They have eyes only for the night, watching, not for the first glimpse of a foe, a shadow that should not be there, a sudden ambush, but for the slow movement of stars across the heavens, the clues that have yet to be gathered, the answers to riddles that they have not yet mastered. They have ears only for the night, listening, not for the sound of the crack of a twig under the foot, not for the whistle coded with notes, not for the rise of a blade, but for the faint echo of one crying out in the distance, for the whisper of some other in the darkness who is speaking to them, who is replying to their words. But they hear only the sounds of the island in the wind, only the sound of the sea making its way to the shore.

They gather knowledge, these star people. They discover. They brave the emptiness, the heights, the winds and the elements for this knowing. They invent anything they can invent that will help them in this quest. Any instrument, any shape, any size.

They exhaust their energies in this thirst for knowledge. They are not afraid. They know nothing is ever lost. For they believe in the motto of their city, in the words that have been uttered over centuries, in the script that speaks to them:

Everything lies somewhere in the night

The City of Constellations:

nothing is ever lost:

not the rainspeak of rainwords in rainfall.
not the words that make your heart tremble.
not the chaos of words, the confusion.
not the words that are red or green or blue or yellow.

not the tango of dancing the rain steps into.
not the compass that points its way towards snow.
not the messages lost between lovers.
not the city buried in sands that time let go.

not the colour of a sky that lies and dreams.
not the armour love wears against the world.
not the echoes of despair.
not the hills, not the valleys. nowhere.

not sadness, not searching, not solitude.
not eulogies written in some forgotten script.
not the rivers that come crying and come crying.
not the name upon his lips.

no, nothing is ever lost.
for the heart of the night does not stop beating.

The Valley

The City of Constellations, the city that hides itself in the darkness from the darkness, so that it may not been seen, the one that knows of the cry of freedom from the City in the Heights but cannot bring itself to scream, is alive in the darkness. Among its inhabitants are the Scribes, the Myth Minders, the Interpreters – the Valley-dwellers. They paint the sky to hold the night. They name the stars so that they may know their flight. They send their words out into the night. They are not afraid of the night for they are used to darkness, and even in this darkness they have light. Starlight. Moonlight. Sunlight. Light that falls from the sky into the valley and below. Light that takes them where they need to go when they leave this city, and cross the island, and go into the ocean. They say to know the stars is to know your way home. So no-one is ever lost. Still, there are many in this city who do not travel the ocean, seldom travel the island, preferring instead the voyages made by imagination and speculation, made by word and myth, made by their great poetries and art. Most of their journeys are in the songs of the stars and in the images of other parts of night. They sing the songs of the seasons, they sing of the river and the moon. They relish the time given them in their city of depths, in their city of deepness, and they discuss much. The winds do not shake them. They do not notice the sound of the sea making its way to the shore. But they keep watch. They watch the stars in the darkness from their darkness.

The Valley-dwellers are sheltered by the mountains that rise above them. They know they are not alone, for at night the lights from the heights introduce them to the stars and tell them where the end of their earth is. And they relish the stars and the darkness the stars find themselves in. For they believe in the motto of their city, in the words they have uttered over centuries, in the cipher that speaks for them:

The heart of the night does not stop beating.

The islands the rain made

It is said that the ocean is a place made of islands in water. Islands the rain made. A scattering of islands as many as the rain could cry, the rain that was wept from the sky, the rain that came from the weeping of one who was alone in the darkness. Each island has the shape of a fallen tear. No-one knows how many tears have fallen. No-one knows how many islands fell, became, existed, and how many are now lost or where they have gone. No-one knows why these islands are no longer seen with the eyes, yet the heart has knowledge of them. It is said that they are like tears of grief. They are sadness fallen from the heart and wept, but, as tears that have fallen are in time no longer seen, so the shape of the islands has been lost. In time.

When the moon is in conversation with the ocean, when the stars eavesdrop, the shapes the islands make melt into a further darkness and then they are only imagined. When the sun comes into the sky and the seas glisten, the ocean becomes like glass and it seems as if the islands have moved from their place of falling and have fallen beneath the waves, or have moved beyond the horizon so that they can no longer be seen, or have given themselves back to the darkness. No-one can find these islands, even though their image is known, even though these tears that have fallen, these islands the rain has made, have names and numbers and shapes.

The shape of the island that holds the Cities of Constellations is one of these fallen tears. But it is a lost tear. It is an island that has not gone beyond the horizon, or perhaps it is the only island that has gone beyond the horizon. It is an island that has not fallen beneath the waves, through there have been times when the waves have been curious about what lies at the heart of the island and have come creeping in, only to leave without that knowledge. For the moon will not let the sea come into the river, for the river is the place that holds all the secrets of her heart, even though each day and night the river makes its way into the sea.

It is an island that has not given itself back into the darkness, even though each night the darkness comes with starry eyes, to claim all that it has cried. For everything belongs to the darkness, even the light. Or, it may be that this is the only island that has given itself back to the darkness and that is why it can find no other, and no other has found this island. This lost tear. This island the rain has made.

The island itself has changed shape through time. The islanders know that the shape of the island has melted, has been changed by the sea, has given itself up to the winds. They know their land is not as it was at the beginning. And they know it changes even as they speak and watch and listen. There was a time when the island did not exist, and the islanders know that a time will come when this island will no longer exist, for it is a tear the sky has cried, and although the weight of grief is great, tears are always lost in time.

The East Wall
The Valley

In the valley there is a road that begins at the harbour and winds its way through the City of Constellations until it reaches the East Wall. Here, one may leave the city by the Gate-of-the-Moon. It bears this name, one of its many names, not for its colour, not for its shape, but because as one stands at this gate, as one contemplates leaving the city by this road, one sees the moon stand proud against the utter darkness. And all who live in the City of Constellations know that pride comes before a fall. They see the moon stand above another city, a city on the heights, a city so close to the sky it seems as if it has claimed the moon, for the moon lingers there, as if listening. As if intent on something or someone.

But the Valley-dwellers know the heart of the moon and they turn their eyes away and look to the stars.

There are not many from the city in the depths who will travel this road. Most of the Valley-dwellers, whose home is almost hidden, do not leave their city by any road at all. And this road is a road that leads only to one place and nowhere else. It is a road that runs through the darkness of a land that can no longer be seen, that winds its way upwards, and keeps going. It does not stop until it reaches the city gates. It does not stop until it brings you to the City of Constellations. The City of the stillness of nightshapes. It is a road that leads to the moon.

Of those Valley-dwellers who do leave their city, there are some who sail upon the ocean. They have been given the name of End-dwellers, and they are a harbour people who love the sea and make ships the colour of the moon. And there are those Valley-dwellers who live at the far edge of the city, the edge that always looks at the mountain, the furthest part of the city from the sea, who are given the name Riparian, because they are a people who love the river. They travel other roads, at midnight. But those who live at the highest point of the city – a place where they are no longer hidden from the night, from the stars, from the winds, a place where the city stands above the earth and clambers into the valley – it is those, the Few, who venture along the road that goes only to one place, the road that climbs up into the mountain, the road that leads to the moon.

...but they do not know why
The Heights.

At night the City on the Heights looks silver. In the day the City on the Heights looks gold. The Few, who venture up to the city by the road that goes nowhere else, begin their journey when the city looks gold. They end their journey at the gates of a city of silver, a city the colour of the moon.

In this City on the Heights the night is full of stars. It is a place full of star-names, each road is called for a constellation, each person has the surname of a star. This is the home of the Loxians.

This is the home of those who know they are of the night, and do not hide from it. They want to know the secrets the darkness holds for them. And darkness waits for the imagination of those who would know.

Theirs is a city of great excitement, for there is always some new discovery, some knowledge uncovered, some riddle finally solved. But there are many enigmas in the night, and the Loxians know this. One answer is given them and another question opens. For sometimes the stars say nothing. But the Loxians embrace everything of the sky. Everything light shines upon, everything darkness reveals.

For they are a people who open their hearts to the night. Their song is of the night. It is a song that can be heard across the island, and even out into the sea. It is carried on the winds. It echoes through the valley. And more than this, they send their words out into the darkness, out into the night. But it is a song of both beginning and ending. And as they sing, it brings a longing into their hearts for something they cannot have, they cannot remember, they do not know, yet they know more than their own heartbeat. It is a quest for something that is lost.

And they sing, but they do not know why.

The Song of the Loxians

Leaving the City of Constellations by the quiet road of the valley, you come to the colour green. Field after field, tree after tree, green stretches itself out. Here and there a small surprise of red or violet or yellow. Above green, the sky lends itself; sometimes carving out the shape of blue, sometimes lying down in clouds of grey, a grey of subtle change-shapes, change-shapes that come and go and will not be still. Sometimes the sky is only the colour of night.

The Riparians, those who live at the East Wall of the City, on the outskirts, have many names for the colours of earth and sky. They have many names for the road that takes them from the city through the meadows and down to the river. It is their custom. It is their desire. Everything and everyone has many names. So, the road you take on leaving the city could be the Long-Road-to-the-River or the Path-that-steps-into-the-Moon or the Road-that-takes-you-to-where-the-Moon-hides. But it is the same road, no matter which name you know it by. It is common to all Valley-dwellers, this wish to call each thing and place and person by more than one name. It is their desire.

It is because they so love their words that they can fill the darkness with moving shapes – the mark that has no end but turns around and goes into itself, the line that wants to go on into the endlessness, the words that find themselves falling over the end of a page, the deep colour of the sound of an echo that fades and can be seen no more, as if written in the alabaster inks of winter. It is because they so love their words that they can fill the darkness with a continual softness, with a flow of phrase, with a moving fantasy, with a life of imagination that cannot stop dancing and cascading. They make their world one of soft, round, deep words that roll in on themselves and then fall far into the night. They make their words so that they always want write, to speak, to lay their hands upon a page, to hear the sounds their symbols make, to discover, to search. They say their words the way a bird that can say everything for everyone, cannot resist the calling of so many voices and must sing. They sing vowels of viridian, they sing syllables of obsidian. They sing their every utterance with colour and shape and the deep expression of the night.

Yet there is one sound that is not their own and which their hearts yearn to have. It is a sound that comes not from their city, not from the voice of the winds as they play with the leaves, not from the toll of a bell that echoes from the ocean, not from the exotic enticements of birdsong. It comes not even from the sighs of the river as it runs through the valley. No, the sound they most love comes from the heights of their island. It is the sound of the Song of the Loxians. It is a sound that awakens in the Valley-dwellers a strange feeling, one they cannot know yet one that is more familiar to them than their own heartbeat.

It is a song that is sung only to the darkness. For the Loxians know that they are children of night, the night that surrounds them, that the stars have fallen into each of their hearts, that they should never be afraid of the darkness they have come from. It is a song in which the Loxians let their words fly like arrows into the heart of the night. And it awakens in the hearts of all the Valley-dwellers a longing that brings them to the edge of tears, because it is the song of both the beginning and the end.

And so, that is why – although the quiet road has such beauty under the sun; the rejoicing of green, the startled intake of breath at a sudden colour, the sight of a red or a violet or a yellow – the Riparians most love to travel the Road-to-the-River-of-Silver-Fragments at midnight. Then, the stars can be seen and the moon falls into the river and the river echoes into the night and there is a strange awakening in the heart of the Riparians at the sound of something they do not know, at the sound of the song of the night breaking their hearts the way the river breaks the heart of the moon.

The Riparians follow the Road-at-Midnight down through the green which now cannot be seen, passing by rocks that show themselves but say nothing, stepping over stones that tell them the river is close by. Then, they come to the Low-Bridge-where-Night-is-seen. It is a bridge so low that it touches the river, so low that the river can speak to it and roll over it, so low that the river can run its fingers across the lengths of the wood, and feel the smallnesses that hold everything together. It is here that the moon first falls into the river. It is here that her heart breaks into a thousand silver pieces and is carried away. It is here that a Valley-dweller can stand and look down and still see the sky.

The lost words of the Valley-dwellers

In The Book of Above the Valley-dwellers write of love, write of all they love, write of all, of everything. They write of what they know and of what they don't know. They write with their hearts pouring out. Thousands describe Autumn. There are poems on all of the Seasons. And they write what is not even their own, because it stirs within them a feeling they cannot let go of. They write the Song of the Loxians in many different ways, in many different words, with every ounce of longing in their souls.

The Valley-dwellers spend long hours writing one sentence in many different ways. That is why one road can be known by many names, that is why the names a person is given are descriptive and each person is known by more than one name. That is why they do not cease in the translations of Loxian scripts, which they cannot stop themselves from describing. They are convinced that the True Song of the Loxians was written in a time long ago by one of their own, by a Valley-dweller. Though their mouths do not utter it, it is the song of their soul. Therefore it confuses them, it confounds them, it vexes them to think that such sounds should be those of the Loxians. That such sounds should be uttered by those who are primarily concerned with the exchange of information. And so the Valley-dwellers write, and so they write...

They love the visual representation of a sound. They love a mark more a note, a curve as much as a falsetto, a stammer of ink on a page instead of the quiver of a voice in air. There is much dispute amongst them as to the most perfect of the translations, as there is a great fear that the original words can never be truly expressed. Those who scribe words discuss with those who scribe words as to whether any of those who live in this City of Constellations can ever truly describe with the pen the sound of the words of this song. Time and time again they talk. Time and time again they gather to look, to view, to study, to feel, to utter what they feel cannot be said. They have written for many hours, through many darknesses, they have written many versions of the same words. So much so, that now the first translation of the Song of the Loxian has been given its own title. The Song of the First. The Firstwords.

But most prefer to call this first translation by the formal title bestowed upon it – The Lost words of the Valley-dwellers.

The first words

The lost words of the Valley-dwellers sing of an island in a sea of stars.
Sing of the moon in solitude. Sing of the river singing. They say:

We are far from knowing.
The stars sing
the journey of what was
and the earth moves.

Out of night has come the day.
Out of night, our small earth.
We send our words out way
beyond the moon and into darkness.
Our words drift away.
Our words journey to find those who will listen.

We call out into the distance…
We call out into the distance…
We call out into the distance…
We call out into the distance…

Less than a pearl in a sea of stars
we are a lost island in the shadows,
yet our endeavours leave this world
as our dreams gather.
It may be our words become lost.
It may be our words find nothing, find no-one.

We call out into the distance…
We call out into the distance…
We call out into the distance…

We call out into the distance…
We call out into the distance…
We call out into the distance….
We call out into the distance…
We call out into the distance…

But there are more than these words.

This is but one version of many versions. This is but one heart of many hearts. Yet no matter how often it is written, the words all say the same thing. The heart of the Loxian cries out to the darkness. The words of the Valley-dweller are in the heart of the Loxian. And both these peoples on this small island of an earth know that they are lost in a sea of stars, know that this place in which they dwell in the universe is a smallness almost unseen. It is less than a pearl. And this sense of smallness is in the history of their singing, of their words, of all that has been handed down to them through the centuries in speech, in sculpture, in script, in motto, in voice, in song. For everything is found in the night, is sung in the night, is sung to the night.

Though they are of two different cities, a city of heights, a city of depths, still each one knows deep inside his heart that they are both born of the same darkness, of the night that is filled with stars. And so the words of one become the songs of the other. And the voice of one becomes written into the tomes of the other.

It matters not that one city follows the moon and the other the river. For are the moon and the river not united by night? Does the river not know the heart of the moon, and does the moon not run with the river? That is why in their most ancient of songs it cannot be known whether a Loxian or a Valley-dweller wrote the words found in the song of the night:

Our words go beyond the moon.
Our words go into the shadows.
The river sings the endlessness.

We write of our journey through night.
We write in our aloneness.
We want to know the shape of eternity.

Who knows the way it is?
Who knows what time will not tell us?

Mountains, solitude and the moon
until the journey's end?
The river holds the lost road of the sky;
the shape of eternity?

Who knows the way it is?
Who knows what time will not tell us?

Where is the beginning?
Where is the end?
Why did we fall into days?
Why are we calling out into the endlessness?

Who knows the way it is?
Who knows what time will not tell us?

But there are more than these words.

This is but one version of many versions. This is but one heart of many hearts. Yet no matter how often it is written, the words all say the same thing. But the same thing is always a question. And each one knows that as one question is answered, another one becomes. And the question that is always in the heart of each city is this:

Are the lost words of the Valley-dwellers the true song of the Loxians?

The fragments

*

They say long ago, in a time before their island, the maker of darkness wept because he was alone. His tears fell through time until they were caught in the strands of gossamer he had cast, for his tears were great, and he was afraid of what might happen. But many of his tears were not captured by the strands and continued to fall and in falling came into the great ocean that surrounded the island. Here they fell in their brightness and were swallowed up by another darkness.

So the seas of the great ocean and the vastness of night looked at each other. The sea echoed the eyes of night. The night looked into the eyes of the sea, and saw itself, and could not leave. Always, when the sun tires and departs, night comes to look into its own eyes, and weeps.

Just as a sunprint steals a moment of your soul, so the sea had stolen some part of the stars so that they could not return to the sky. But the great ocean cast forth a pearl to console the maker of darkness, and the maker, being moved by the beauty of such a gesture, made it so that the stars became pearls in the darkness.

They say to know the stars is to know your way home, so into the manifest of the island was written each star, each constellation, each pearl, each tear.

*

They say long ago it all began. They say there may not be a beginning. They say there may be many beginnings. They say some day they will know the night. But the night is full of everything. It is everything. It is all they do not know.

*

Sometimes the islanders lose themselves in the stars. They call this experience The Happening. The shapes that are familiar become lost; as leaves are lost in the forest, as stones are lost on the mountainside, as snowflakes are lost in a blizzard. There is nothing more than a million scattered lights, a confusion, and there is no longer a road through the night. In times such as these the islanders do not journey.

*

The Valley-dwellers see the moon splinter in the river, and so they choose the river as their emblem, for it travels where they do not, it is free from the fear of the open space of night and it is strong enough to break the heart of the moon into a thousand different pieces. But there is much they do not know about the river. They do not know it runs through the valley to hide from the sky.

They say that those on the Heights can see the ocean wrap itself around their island. They can see inlets and peninsulas. They can see the land-feathers of sand and rock and the sea edging itself in. They can see mountains and valleys, hillsides and harbours. All on their island. To the north they can see the sea all the way to the horizon. In every direction it is the same. At night they see the stars and the moon.

Those in the Heights choose the moon as their emblem. For the river is a distant thing, and small. It stretches itself into thinness and disappears. It looks frightened. It does not stop talking and muttering and mumbling, and its conversation with the sea often travels to the Heights as those in the Heights turn to listen elsewhere. When the night falls in, it goes hiding. Whereas the moon has no fear. Although the day swallows it, each darkness brings it back again to sit amongst the stars. But there is much they do not know of the moon. They do not know that each night the river breaks the heart of the moon into a thousand silver pieces.

And there is much that neither city knows about the words in the Black Book of the Night.

Those in the Heights have studied the words and yet have not found these places the man speaks of. They know it is a map of a journey, a journey of the heart, yet they seek to find these cities, these roads, these islands, these valleys. They have crossed their ocean, but not so far as to find what they seek, and have come home by the stars. Each journey is an odyssey of nothing, for nothing happens, save sometimes they lose themselves in the stars and their hearts tremble and their breath quickens.

Those in the Valley say that the song of the man is sung from the Valley, for they too travel by emotion, by imagination, they too know the song of their hearts. And the places their journeys arrive at are also in their hearts. For where else can a man search for whom he loves but in his heart?

*

Those in the City of Constellations, the city of the stillness of nightshapes, the city that sits on the Heights, know themselves by the name of erraKan. Their name comes from an ancient word that has almost forgotten its beginning. They say long ago these people called themselves errarheeaKan, which can mean the people from beyond the moon. But their early histories are not fully known, even though they say they know their origins. And, as is the custom of words which are ever moving, ever changing, like a river winding its way to the sea, sounds lose themselves, letters fall over the horizon of the pages and are gone forever.

They say that their first birth was in a place far away, in another part of night. It is here that their history becomes confused, for many of the original writings have been lost, only the few have survived the centuries. Yet those words that have clung to their hearts through time are still sung. Those words are still part of their heart.

*

Those in the City of Constellations, the city of the stillness of nightshapes, the city that lays itself down in the valley, know themselves as erraLuua, the people of the shadows. For they live in a valley of shadows, on an earth that is an island lost in the shadows. This name they give themselves is a name for all Valley-dwellers, even though these people have divided themselves into other names, into many names. The erraEa are the river people of the valley, although others know them by different names. Some call them erraNayllow - those-who-walk-the-road-of-the-night. Some call them Riparian.

The erraRhee are those who love the ocean and travel in ships the colour of the moon. Some call them the End-dwellers, for they live on land that falls into the ocean, land that says goodbye to the island, land that lies and listens to the rhythm of the sea.

And there are many others not yet mentioned. The erraLlay, those who sing. The erraOroommmay, those who write in the way of the Ea, the written water shapes. The Few, those who live in the valley above the valley, who do not live in the darkness yet remain in the shadows, who follow the road that leads to a city of silver and nowhere else. They are also known as errarheeaErrusay, for they live beyond the walls of both cities.

Each of these peoples have many names, but the name they know themselves by is the one closest to their hearts.

...of words that exist...

Darkness, and then light. Rain, and then islands. Seasons, and then singing. And after these, the written breath of the other. All of these things were a long time ago and, before singing, nothing was written. So much is unknown.

On this island the rain made, on this island cried into the ocean, the peoples of the two cities write. They write with words of the beginning that will always be, and with words which now find themselves in flux and in time will not know their beginning and will not remember what they were. They will change their shape the way the island the rain has cried changes shape, in time. And someday they will not be.

And there are words that are yet to come, that lie unwritten.

Of the written words that exist, not only are there many names given to the world and everything in it, not only are there many translations and adaptations of the one song or poem or writing, not only is each person named and then named again, but each word and name is given in six different scripts.

There are six scripts* on this island because each script is written in the hand of a season, and there are six seasons* that the peoples of this island have named for themselves.

The first falls under Essa, the Autumn; it is the script of the winds whose symbols change the way a world changes, or an island, or a word, or the course of the winds themselves. As Autumn ends, the autumnal script is over, and a new script begins. It writes itself in the slow, elaborate, decorative indigo inks of Ju, the Winter, which lie against white, or the alabaster inks of Winter which hide themselves in the colour of snow, so that sometimes their contours cannot be seen.

The season of Ea, the third season of the island, is that of the river, and it brings forth the hidden water shapes. For when the heart of snow melts, many tears are shed. This season lies close to the words given by the rain, the sky-crying symbols that represent the new season of Pirrro, the Spring. Sometimes it cannot be told which are the tears that fall from the heart and which are the tears the sky has been crying.

Luua, the Summer, always writes itself in shadow, which the gold of the sun nestles next to and desires. The last season, the time of Kan, is the time of the archer script, the feathered symbols, the shape of the moon. It is but a matter of days. And it is a strange season, for it is divided. It falls at the beginning of every other season. And so it is throughout the year, appearing and disappearing, coming and going, being and not being. Kan is always with another season the way the moon is with a wanderer.

He is one of those, looking...

Here, in the midst of the sea, is the City of Constellations. There are two cities who claim this name. They stand on an island, one that throws its hands up to the skies and aspires. There are only two cities on this island; one which sits above the highest point of the island and one below the valley, deeper than the lowest point in the island. If you follow the road to the heights you come to the City of Constellations. If you follow the road to the valley you come to the City of Constellations. Each claims to be the most ancient, and therefore the original holder of the title. It is a strange argument when both cities know only of each other, of their island, of the size of the sky.

Even in their great ocean they have found no other. Yet both claim to have named the stars, to know the origin of themselves. Both give different histories to the stars, and call the constellations by their own appellations. That is why there is confusion on the island, and why those who live in the valley are cautious of those who live in the Heights, and why those who live on the heights look down upon the Valley-dwellers and doubt them.

There is only one name they both agree on, and it is given to the most insignificant star in their sky. It is a star which can barely be seen. One almost has to close their eyes to hold it steady in their sight. It is called The Pearl. And it is a constellation of one. A unique constellation. It is accepted as such because of its position in the sky, for it is the only star that is truly surrounded by darkness. And this area of darkness is called The Secret. All others of the night are with each other is some shape or form or fashion. But The Pearl is just that; one small precious light, alone in the secret darkness.

It is more truly named than the islanders realise. Because it is a tear of the maker it is as important as all others stars. But it is more than this. It truly is in the midst of a secret. How could the islanders know, as they discuss time and signs and mysteries and theories, that this star is a star of life?

Around it life in its various forms flourishes. And of all the myriad lives that have come and gone through time, that come and go, there is, at this very moment, one who wanders a world made possible by The Pearl, one who carries within him a great sadness. It is a sadness in his heart, so not all can see it, it is a sadness searching, endlessly, for the love it has lost, it is a man searching for his heart, for a love he cannot find. It is a man wandering through cities he does not know, arriving on island after island and leaving and still going on, searching for iquate roads, invious places. It is a man seeking what cannot be. It is a man searching for the one he loves, and has lost. He is one of those, looking…

Part two

Water shows the hidden heart

The wanderer

Fixed stars, and then everything moving. Seven, they said, and then nine. Nine wanderers following a star. Nine wanderers moving through the darkness. Some had many moons, moons they would not let go of, moons they caught and held in their gaze. Some had some moons, moons that went with them as they journeyed, that held their hands. And one, one had one moon, its brightness in the night moving with it, moving it. Everything moving, even the earth, for the earth does not stand still, no matter what they said. It lay a perfect distance from its star, this earth, so that around this sun, around this pearl in the darkness, upon this wanderer - a wanderer.

On this earth he set out, the wanderer, on this planet we name for ourselves. On this earth, this man went searching. His was an invisible quest, the quest for a love he had lost. The quest for love over death.

He could not believe that her life was over, that who she was was no more. That her laughter would no longer be heard, that her soft words would no longer armour him against the world, that her eyes would no longer consume him and that he would no longer be able to hold the one who had loved him so much. Five thousand days they had travelled together, and now she was gone.

It was a cross he could not bear. It was a burden he could not shoulder. And so he sought her in invisible places, that she might once again be with him, laughing, stepping over puddles the rain had made, loving him. He created images from his memory, he imagined, he walked in circles, hour after hour, day after day, aimlessly, not knowing why.

And as the earth travelled through the night, he began a journey. The route he mapped within his heart. It would take him to places he would remember and places he did not know. He relegated cities, islands, plains, valleys, mountains, to his deepest emotions, to his confusion and loss, to his despair, to his love. All the secret moments he had let go became places he now named. All that had happened he turned into cities – cities he made to be strong, so that they might fortress his love. All of his desires he made into forms, like flowers, that might bloom and be again. Invisible places where memory and hope would be his guides, his guardians, his saviours. He created these images, he imagined. And then he walked, this man looking for whom he loves.

But he did not know why.

The Place of Rains

At the Place of Rains the one-who-is-looking-for-whom-he-loves arrives. It is a divided place, for it depends on how you view the rain how this city will seem to you. It is the same place, it is the same rain, but one part of the city is a place of sorrow; heavy, tear-laden, overcast, dull. It seems as if there is no bright thing. There is only a constant sound that does not separate night from day, nor hour from hour. It is hard to tell from the light that falls through the window just what part of the day is happening outside. The morning is as gray as the afternoon, the afternoon is as dim as the evening, the evening is as dark as the night. Neither sun nor moon are observed, nor are the stars seen, for this place lies under the domain of clouds, and they dominate everything. They accumulate in great numbers, so much so that the multitudes of clouds are seamless and appear as one continuous, uninterrupted sky. Each individual cloudshape lies undistinguished, for everything is lost in the commingling. It is like an atlas of nowhere, this sky. A map of lost places, over which there is much weeping.

On the other side of the same city there is a great beauty, and it is found in the sound of the rain as it sings on the rooftops and dances its way joyfully through the streets until it meets itself, and then falls apart, each of its hearts touching the ground and exploding with excitement. It is a harmony unlike any other, yet it is heard over and over again. Sometimes it is like an orchestra whose minims and quavers, whose semi-quavers fall from the sky. Sometimes it is like the sound of a tango rejoicing in its own steps. Sometimes it is like a slow sea that has come to tell you nothing, and comes again and tells you nothing, and tells you nothing at all. But there is a great beauty in each drop that falls, for each one shines like the eyes of a woman in love, and they sparkle.

And as he walks into this place he remembers the eyes of a woman in love. And he knows that in the sound of the rain is the sound of his tears, for his tears fall in the rain, singing. Their threnody is his alone, for he is alone. And he knows all too well the sound of his own weeping.

Many times he had been to this city. Each time the many steps of the rain came to him, dancing, and did not stop. It was the beat of his heart that he heard in the rain. It was the rhythm of love, and so he would lie and listen and imagine.

They had been joyful visits to this place, for she was with him. He was amused watching her avoid the puddles. Intrigued when she observed herself in a mirror of raindrops. Laughed when she opened her arms to the skies. And each drop that fell reflected her eyes, and her eyes were the eyes of a woman in love. And they sparkled.

This time he entered this place alone. He entered half-way between the joy of the rain and its sadness. He could hear the laughter of girls running, avoiding puddles, opening their arms to the skies. He could see the rain tango. He could see the downpouring of tears, the light trying to find its way in through the windows, the grief of a sky whose heart had been broken.

Now, like the rain, he did not stop. He kept walking. He let the sounds pass through him and disappear. He no longer looked to see if, in each raindrop, the eyes of a woman in love sparkled. He did not veer to the right. He did not turn to the left. He walked on through the middle regions until there were no more tears falling, and the sky could find itself again and the clouds fell apart, each into its own shape.

The City of indecisions and hesitations

He was not sure he had entered the city by the right road. He was not sure at all. Although he had been here before the city looked different, as it always does. For the city changes from moment to moment as the stones it is made of are the stones of doubt and indecision and hesitation. It cannot be otherwise. And so he watched the rise and fall of all before his eyes, and wondered where he should go, and what he should do.

He had come by the one road he knew, the route he had come before. But any road will lead you to this city, though each road brings you to a different point within the walls. You can never be sure it is not the same point you would have arrived at anyway, even if you had come by another road.

Doubt enters the mind as soon as a man walks through the city gates.

There are no street maps, there is no atlas of this great place. There are no names for the streets, for nobody knows whether a street will be or not, nor which street they stand on, nor if it is the same street it was a moment ago. They do not know which road they should or should not follow, or if they have already made the wrong choice. Perhaps they should have chosen another route? And so everything changes with this thought.

In his sadness and desperation the one-who-is-looking-for-whom-he-loves had come to this city, not knowing how he had arrived, not knowing why he was there. He did not know where to go within the city, he did not know how to leave it.

Although there are city walls there are no boundaries, for this city spreads far beyond its original gates. There are no signs. There is only one thing in the whole of the city that is familiar to everyone.

THE CITY OF INDECISIONS AND HESITATIONS

Everywhere is written and scratched onto the stones of doubt the same words, the same phrases - and they made his heart tremble and his breath quicken.

He knew this was a place he did not want to stay, yet he could not leave. If only he had known that it did not matter which road he chose to leave the city by. Instead, he wondered if each road eventually met outside the city gates and you arrived at the next city anyway, no matter which road you took. Perhaps there were innumerable possibilities. Perhaps it made no difference at all. He did not know.

All he knew was that he would not find her there.

Once again he passed by the large blocks of stone. Once again he saw the words that were written. Once again his heart quivered and his step quickened. And so, as all who live in this city or who sojourn or linger, he hesitated, he debated, he could not decide. He wandered the streets he did not know but could not find his way back to the beginning nor onto the end.

There are as many gates leaving the city as there are entering. Above each of these is carved the city's motto. But this is a city unlike any other. It has not just one motto, it has many. And to confound the indecisive man still further, the carvings move just as the stones of all the buildings move, so that a man can never truly know which road he chooses. Having studied the words and decided on his route, he may find that as he passes through the gates he is already on the wrong road, or on a road that he has not chosen; that has been chosen for him by fate or chance or by a moment of indecision or doubt.

The one-who-is-looking-for-whom-he-loves stood for a while and took in the view of the city gates, and read the words that rose above them, and his heart trembled and his breath quickened. They were the same words, the same phrases he had seen everywhere within the city walls scratched onto the stones of doubt.

And the words tumbled from his mouth as he read each one, for he already knew them in his heart:

"What if…"

"Will the same fate happen?"

"What is shaped, shall be"

"Often the road a man travels to avoid his fate is the very one that brings him to it"

"Maybe…"

"Maybe not…"

Finally, in confusion, he walked through the city gates. He walked through without looking up to find out which words he was passing under. After all, it may be that all roads will meet and bring him to the next city. But would it be a different city than the one it should have been?

Although he had chosen before his first step, he knew that by the time he had passed through the gate, there was every chance the words would change…

Maybe.

Maybe not.

The Island of the house-the-colour-of-the-sea

To the north of the island lies only the sea. It is the sea until it falls over the edge of the horizon, and even after this it is the still the sea. It is a lonely vision to the north, its only company is the raise of waves in the wind.

But to the south there is the soothing aspect of sand. Golden, even without the sun. It is wound round the bay until it cannot be anymore.

To the east and west of the island lies land, land that stretches out its hands to feel the sea, to let the water run through its fingers, to touch the waves, to know that it is not alone with its burden of earth. It finds comfort in the sound of the sea. It finds freedom and repose.

The sea combs itself around the island. The waves murmur. They question and answer themselves. And then, for a moment, something other than the sea is heard. Sighs and whispers. Whispers and sighs from the island. Whereas the sea says nothing, the sighs from the island say everything, and always.

Yet no-one goes to the island anymore. There is nothing there, nothing but the ruins of a house or a church or a sentinel. Nothing but stones and the grass that comes creeping until it can creep no more. Nothing but leaves that disturb the night when they shout in the wind. Nothing but granite and ancient graffiti.

Where once there were words given to the air, now there are scrawls on stone. At the edge of a cliff, on a standing stone, words have been written. But they themselves no longer know what they say. They have etched themselves into the earth when others have been given to the air. But now they are as lost as any spoken word.

They stand alone. No-one has knowledge of them any more.

On a hard ridge of granite there are marks sculpted into the bones of the earth. Marks made by someone, sometime. It is not known why they were made. It is not known whether they are a name, or a route, or the mention of a life.

On a stone laid flat as if its only purpose was to lie and look at the sky, someone has scrawled what seems to be a message to the stars. But no-one knows why this should be. No-one knows what the stars once saw.

These words have made mysteries endure. Mysteries that belong to the Island-of-the-house-the-colour-of-the-sea. Nobody knows if it was truly a house, or why it is no longer there. No-one knows that it was not a sentinel or what it saw. Nobody knows if it was a church or a sacrifice to the stars, and what it meant. But they know that the same words written on stone are heard in the winds. They know that this place they call the Island-of-the-house-the-colour-of-the-sea is a place where tears fall as often as the waves come to visit the shore, which is always. But whereas the sea says nothing, the sighs from the stones say the same words over and over again.

The Place of Momentoes

He left a kiss.

He gave a part of himself to the earth.

Where others had left some token of themselves, some show of affection and regard, he left only the sign of his love in the air.

Where others had written words on tear-stained pages, had gathered blossoms of red and white, he had given the greatest part of his heart.

Where others had placed objects of desire upon this altar, he was crucified by love. And bore it. But no-one could see how much he had given.

So much is spoken without words, more than may be understood.

So much is shown in the gesture, rather than in the placing of gold and silver.

So much was in his heart.

He gave a part of himself to the earth.

He left a kiss.

The Valley of lost time

Down in the valley a bell rings out. It rings out not the hour, but time that has been lost, so that a mournful peal is heard long before one reaches the point on the mountain road that descends into this place. It is heard second by second, as that is how time is lost, and the peal from one second echoes into the next, so that it sounds like a carillon, rather than one lone bell. It tells of hours and days and years that have been stolen or taken from a man. It tells of hours and days and years that a man has neglected or that have been abandoned by him. It is a sound that does not cease.

A slow, winding road takes a man into this valley. It is a slow, winding road so that a man has time to reflect, to consider, to remember, and to ponder the place he is about to enter.

All that is in this valley is the bell tower. Four-sided, it has four clocks. These clocks have no hands, for there is no need to tell the time, it has already been lost. These clocks need no mechanisms for they do not need winding. They do not go forwards or backwards. They do not go fast or slow. They do not keep time.

It is as if time has been left standing, the way a man who enters this valley feels he is left standing. It is as if the clocks reflect what is not there, so that a man is given to knowing what is gone and what yet may be. For as a man travels through this valley he becomes aware of what he has lost. He sees clearly those moments he would like to live again so that he may make them blossom into fullness, rather than let them wither and die. He sees clearly his own sadness at what has been taken from him, through no fault of his own.

The erumpent form of the bell tower is the only visible thing in the valley besides the grass. There are no trees to distract the mind when the winds blows. There are no flowers to distract the eyes from the verdure, from the one colour. There are no birds singing or quarrelling or in display, so that the ears only hear the sound of the bell.

Nothing runs across the field, frightened. Nothing hunts or argues or despairs. There is no river telling of where it's going, telling of where it's not going. No other stones keeping the histories. All that is in the valley is the bell tower. Ringing.

It takes each man a different span of time to cross the valley. But he follows a path well worn in contemplation. What each man sees on the face of the clock is known only to him. What each man hears in the lament of the bell is known only to him.

For nothing can truly tell a man what he has lost, except his heart.

The City of End and Endlessness

On entering this city you stand at its edge, against the abyssal darkness, yet you cannot tell where the city ends. It seems as if it has spread out its fingers, as if it cannot stop reaching out, searching, feeling, moving out to find what is beyond itself, and beyond that, if anything else is.

It is a city of awe and confusion, of discussion and discourse, of theories and beliefs, of minds opening and closing, of possibilities and impossibilities. It is a city written as an enigma, waiting for the imagination of man. It is a city of night set alight with furies, accidents, realisations. It is a city where dark angels move, wingless, through the invisible, until they meet their doom.

Some day this city would no longer know his heartbeat, the way it had forgotten hers. Some day he would not be, and his heartbeat would be lost in the immensity. He wanted to let go of this world, the way she had let go, but time was not yet ready. While he moved, she moved, but he could not see her. When he spoke, she spoke, but he could not hear her. But he heard the murmur of the breeze as it opened the flowers and wandered through the fields, touching the grass, whispering. And he felt the soft winds touch his face and play with his hair.

Everything seemed to be within this city. Everything, except the answers to the enigma. Day by day man was beginning to decode, to understand, yet he remained confused. And day by day he wondered if the answers were not to be found in the night.

And the one-who-is-looking-for-whom-he–loves also looked to the night, and wondered. But the night gave him no answers. Just another enigma. And he despaired. Just as death was as frightening as the eternity of life, the not-being as terrifying as the forever, so it was with where he now stood, with this place he found himself in, with where he was.

But in this city of end and endlessness how could it be otherwise?

The Isle of Revenants

The waves are getting ready for everywhere and all at the same time. They do not know what gives them their restless nature, but they cannot stop themselves in their endless quest. They do not know what they are looking for, only that it has not yet been found.

Sometimes they feel as if they have grasped the reason for their anxious departures, only to have it wash through their fingers and lose itself. They feel as if they are nowhere, and must keep going, until they are somewhere they do not know, but they know they will recognise it when they have arrived. But they never arrive. They just keep going to and fro, to and fro, back and forth, back and forth, much like those who find themselves on the Isle of Revenants. They too travel back and forth, to and fro, east and west, west and east, east and west.

When those on the island stand at its eastern shore looking out over the sea, over the restless waves, waves as restless as their own souls, they see the beauty of the sun as it lies down on the hillside and as it brightens the grass. They see green as they have never seen it before. They hear the barking of dogs in the distance and the laughter of children ripple the air. They hear the echo of a bell, which echoes against itself until it sounds like a host of bells ringing. They remember when the berries brought forth their beautiful colours and became jewels in the sun. They remember the scent of the purple hyacinth, the flower of sorrow, seeking to be forgiven. They remember the white hyacinth, the flower of beauty. The blue hyacinth, which embodies constancy. They remember both sadness and joy but their hearts are unsettled. And they say to themselves: "What I seek must be in the west".

When those on the island stand on its western shore looking out over the sea, over the restless waves, waves as restless as their own souls, they see a canvas of ever changing colour. They see the reflection of the sky looking down into blue eyes, the warm chaos of gold and yellow and orange as the sun falls into the sea, the gray tones of sadness that cover the waves. They see the stars mesmerized by the sea which is mesmerized by the stars. They see the moon looking for love and, in its madness, letting the ocean pull its heart apart, until it dawns upon the moon, and the moon pulls its heart back from the ocean. They see the immensity of night as it tries to find itself. In all of these episodes there is no sound other than the sea. And those on the island who stand looking out, see and hear these wonders, but their hearts are unsettled. And they say to themselves: "What I seek must be on the eastern shore"

This is the way it always was; that which was distant was worthy and desirable because it was distant, that which they have here, which they hold in their hands, is nothing, because it is here, in their hands.

Without the great journey to seek what is not known, they cannot be fulfilled. The leaf of a tree with an exotic name must surely be more prized than this one green leaf that falls before them as the autumn approaches. Besides, where the sun lies down on the hill is much more beautiful than this shore they now stand on.

They search for what cannot be, and they cannot stop searching.

To be at peace they must give themselves up to what is, the way the waves must let themselves be at peace with the sea. But it does not happen.

The City of Solitudes

What can be said of the City of Solitudes other than that each man is alone in his heart. That each man, though he stands in the midst of a million other men, is a solitude unto himself. And in this solitude there are those who put out their hands. They build bridges. They make roads. They carve pathways into even the most difficult terrains. All of these bridges and roads and pathways lead away from themselves. Yet they lead to other solitudes. All needing somewhere to go, someone to go to. There are those who raise their voice so that the wind will carry their words into the aloneness of another heart, and that heart will hear them and come searching, calling to them, answering. There are those who spell their hearts into existence, who write the deeper desire of their being, so that all will know their solitude. There are those who do not know their aloneness, who are not fully aware, and yet hear the faint echo of voices, or glance at the shapes indigo makes on a page, or sing when others sing, so there is no sound of aloneness. And there are those who know their own solitude, and know each man's solitude, and know that even the wind loses itself and the mountains come and go as every other in this span of time.

One always enters this city alone, even though there may be others to greet them. One always leaves this city alone. Within its walls, all life happens. Yet it is as if the one-who-is-looking-for-whom-he-loves has always been in this city, has never left it, even though he has travelled mile upon mile, has put his foot in the places love fell, has existed in another's heart. As if through years of distance all those miles pull themselves back into this one inch of earth, back to this place.

He, too, had built bridges. Not with his hands, not with brick or mortar or steel, but with his eyes open and his heart stretched out until it could go no further. He, too, had made roads, not with sweat falling from his brow, but with his understanding. He, too, had forged pathways through many difficult terrains, not with axe or saw, but with his hope. And these roads and bridges and pathways had followed routes he did not know of, had not dreamt of, never knew existed. Until he had arrived. For all roads lead somewhere, to someone. And his roads lead to her.

How often they had let go their words into the winds, not understanding life, not understanding death. How often they had taken the flow of indigo into their hands and told each other of their deeper desires. Echo of voices, shapes on pages. Singing. And those moments of knowing: the epiphanies of mountain, wind, cloud, ocean. The song of the sands sung by a million, million different voices, their hearts broken and broken again, until the one heart had become many and their wanderings that of each man in this city of solitudes.

This is truly the City of Cities. It is a place alone, yet it covers the atlas of the world and further.

The City of the Distance-from-you

The City of the Distance-from-you is any city, is every city. It is found on any island, on every island, surrounded by ocean, by oceans. It falls into a valley, the way a river falls and comes crying, tears, all tears. It is closed in by mountains, any mountain, all mountains. It is reached by any road, every road, everywhere.

It needs no compass. It lies towards the north in deep snow, in light snow, in snow that has its own name. It lies towards the south, it is a city in the sands; the sands of deserts, the sands of the shore, the sands of time. It lies towards the east and can be walked through by moonlight, and in the midnight it is lit with many candles, and then the afterglow of embers. It lies towards the west, it is a city on stilts, it is a city following the undulation of hills, it is a city that looks both backwards and forwards and in every other direction.

It is a city of seasons, one season, all seasons. It is a city blown cold by brumal breathings, whose hands chill in the winter. It is sprung green by spring, it is dressed in vernal petticoats. It is painted to accommodate the summer; chrysal colours, the richness of reds, rubicelle, violet, the prettiest pinks. It is a city fallen into autumn, which readies itself for loss.

It is a city full of passion, of heartbeats. It does not stop dancing. From this city manuscripts of song arise. Laughter is heard. Desire follows the streets. It is a city angry at itself, it does not stop shouting. There is a chaos of words, a confusion, a cacophony of every sound the soul can make. It is a city in sadness, it cannot explain its heartache and grief, there are pages of tears everywhere. It is a city of hope, and hope has strong wings so it may carry itself to the place where gods cherish the soul of man.

THE CITY OF THE DISTANCE-FROM-YOU

It is a city of secret moments. It is a secret city of moments. It is a city secret in moments.

The City of the Distance-from-you is a dream, or it is here, now, in this moment, in this place. It is a city he remembers, the one-who-is-looking-for-whom-he-loves, for it is a city the distance from her, and the distance from her is more than miles.

The City of Words of blue and yellow and green and red

He comes to a place he has been before. It is the City of Sentiments, a city of gardens and flowers, a city of blues and yellows and greens and reds in the shape of leaves, in the pattern of petals. A city of heady aromas and soft scents. A city of sylvan language and floral speech. A city of gestures.

He knows that on entering this place he will choose a flower, the way elsewhere one would choose a road to follow or a direction that catches the eye. Most people choose what is in their hearts. A man in sadness gathers in his hands a feuillemort of dead leaves, whereas a man in love chooses a blossom of rose or myrtle or violet. A creative man will pick an imagination of lupins and a compassionate man a bouquet of elderflower or a kindness of bluebell. Some choose the blossom of the almond for it is the symbol of hope, and they come with a prayer in their hearts. He knows only too well that all flowers are of the moment, that the blossoms change as the heart changes, so he does not delay in his choice.

You may enter this city in red and leave in blue. You may enter this city with anger and leave with innocence. You may enter this city in despair and leave in hope. Or you may enter this city through the heath of solitude and leave through the heath of solitude, as may sometimes happen.

The last time he had come to this city, he had held her hand in his hand, they had walked together through the perfumed streets. Together they had chosen the rose and the violet, which are of love. They had spent a long time in this place, in fact, the rest of her life. But she left this city without him and he left this city alone. Now, on this arrival, he chose not only the red rose but the pheasant's eye for his sorrowful remembrances, and phlox because, although they were separated, their souls were together, untied, united, still as one. And always, the forget–me–not, which is true love.

As nothing can be hidden in this city, each stranger who passes him by, shares with him a moment of his sadness, for those who pass through this place learn compassion, as each man's garden reveals his heart. A person with avarice within him will attract the auricole, and it will thrive in his garden and overgrow, and he will not be able to cut it down, unless he first cut the avarice out of his heart. And those who have been unfaithful in love are spelt in yellow and given the shape of the rose. And those they have hurt know the thorn of this rose. Those forsaken have a garden filled with anemones. And those who try to conceal their love cannot do so, for the acacia will say to everyone that which has not been spoken, and the althea will proclaim the intensity of their emotion. Anger too abides in this language, it is expressed in the deep red and crimson of the peony.

Deeds are still done, and thoughts are still thought. Such revelation does not stop love or hope or ambition or hate. Everything is told to everyone in words of blue or yellow or red or green. Syllables are shaped like petals. Histories and futures are told in leaves and begin and end in a blade of the grass. The seasons exist all in the one day, and each day can be summer and winter, spring and autumn.

And so the one-who-is-looking-for-whom-he-loves passed through the many gardens of the city and, where he paused and waited a while and remembered, the blossoms of the trumpet flower appeared, and his eyes would fill with tears, for these flowers told him what was in his heart.

And still he walked through the city, every place he could think of, every mile, every inch. But he did not find her. And his sadness looked out at the world but he could not speak. The tears that had fallen from him fell on all he had gathered in his hands: dead leaves, forget-me-nots, a bough of yew, and tears from Persia, the mourning iris. Amongst these sorrows, as if in blessing, two poppies, one red and one white. These are the flowers of the consolation of sleep and the sleep of the heart.

The City of Sleep

It is here that he seeks refuge. Having travelled eternities to find her, he has come to a city of hills and valleys, where one can meet everyone and no-one. The streets come and go as they please. There is no reason to give them a name. Each person knows the street by his own name, so that each street has a million different names. Buildings are risen and then they do not exist. Suddenly you can find yourself within a garden, one you know, one you don't know. Suddenly you find yourself on the western shore looking east whereas the moment before you were on the eastern shore looking west. One moment you are looking at a multitude of stars and the next you are looking at a pearl in the darkness and you see how small your earth is, so small that you can barely see it, so small that you almost have to close your eyes to know it's there.

Nowhere on earth is there a city that does not bear this name. They are numerous, these cities, as numerous as poppy seeds which give themselves over to the winds and fly to places they do not know, to those who do not yet know them.

And these cities are cities of many regions, many mansions, many dreams. There also exists within them some remnant of time you do not quite remember, some part of time that has not been, something you do not know.

It is here that he seeks refuge. Having travelled from the City of Words of blue and yellow and red and green, and not having found her, having left with the flowers of sleep and consolation, he at last lies down.

And he dreams.

He dreams the far western shore where the last legs of the land give way to the ocean. Here the wind will hold you in its arms. Will cradle you. You can give your body to the wind, and it will bear you. Here the winds will not let you fall because their arms are strong and wide and their hearts are open. It is a place to hear words you do not understand, and yet you know what they are telling you…

And he dreams.

He dreams of comfort and repose. He dreams the eternal moment. He dreams his heart is frozen in time with hers, and they know of nothing else, and they know no-one, and this is the eternal moment. It is their scripture. It is what should be. It is love.

And he dreams.

He dreams her touch, her smell, her voice. He dreams the mornings when sunlight fell into their room, and wound itself over them and covered them, the way he covered her. He dreams the shadows they lay into when they would lie and look at the sky and wonder. He dreams her, and the way she laughed in the rain, the way she avoided the puddles, the way she looked into the raindrops to see her own love sparkle. For she loved him, and he knew this.

And he dreams.

He dreams her, and the way her hair came crying over her shoulders. He dreams his own shoulders, where her head lay, where her tears could comfort themselves. He dreams their dreams, those that became, and those that can never be.

And in his dreaming he hears the soft murmurs of voices, as one would hear the sea, the sea that comes to you and tells you nothing, the sea that tells you nothing at all. Yet it is as if these voices have something to say. The way the winds carry words you do not understand. And he opens his heart to hear them. And he listens.

He dreams the winds, and the winds come to him and say...

Where the scent of love lies, sleeping

There was a time when he did not know her touch, nor the way her hair came crying over her shoulders, nor the scent of her, nor the nape of her neck, hidden, passionate, waiting. He had not known the vermilion of her lips and her eyes knew nothing of him.

There was a time when she did not know him, could not fathom his texture of jaw, had not measured his shoulders, did not glimpse herself in his eyes. She had not known the stride of him nor his fearlessness in love. She had not known his hands.

Then everything came together in a trembling kiss. How his shoulders surrounded her, how the nape of her neck revealed itself. How his eyes followed her, the way the curve of a road follows the river. He followed her over the rib's ridge and into where the syllables fall and echo. This is where the scent of love lay, sleeping.

Tonight, he has a memory of a kiss. Of kisses. Trembling against her skin. Trembling on the contours of his lips, moving over her. He has a memory of hair falling down over her shoulders, dark like the night, soft as wishes. He has a memory of clothes, unrobed. Of moonlight, falling onto love. Tonight, he dreams moonlight.

Tonight, he dreams a day. A day when the summer came to them and they lay in the long grass and closed their eyes. The sound of everything was in the air, the sound of everything in the day, everything said and sung and shouted came over the trees and through the song of the long grass and into their hearts. Bells were heard, and the slow distance of a train. Birds stirred everywhere and the sound of man occasionally echoed. Eyes closed, they opened into everything in the day and they lay and let the soft perfume of verbena, the flower of emotion, meander over them. Which of its colours had sent forth this scent they did not know. These sweetnesses were given to them by the hands of the most gentle god, Zephyrus, the west wind, who could never resist the fragrance of his love, the flower. The flower, she who gave everything to him. He carried her scent, and that part of her, far into the world, over fields, across inches, to where her heart would blossom and grow once more and she would not stop being.

And more than this fell over them. The warmth of the sun came down upon them and for a while there was no worry, no apprehension, no disturbance. Simply the being. Simply the moment. It was a moment of breathing, of the rhythm of breathing, of the touch of breath. It was a moment that might be forever. It was a moment that was apart from the world. It was a moment dreamt without end. Their dreaming. Their endlessness. There is an echo of words which says that nothing lasts forever. But while the memory of this moment is in his heart, then it will still be. For surely everything lies somewhere in the night.

Tonight, he has a memory of her footprints in the sand. They had been walking all day along the shore. She had collected shells. Shells that had left the sea. Shells abandoned by the sea as it followed the moon. Shells that would not speak to the sea anymore. Other islands find a fragile moon, she had said. She had collected seeds that had drifted on the ocean from some place unknown, and found themselves here, on this shore, in her hand. They had strange names, they were silent about their origins. Once, it was thought they belonged to the sea. Once, it was thought they arose from some fabulous underwater tree. Description after description had befallen these distance-drifters, these peregrine seeds. They were amulets, protectors, mysteries. But on this day, on this shore, she had gathered them. They were seeds that had travelled oceans and they reminded her of love, because only love would set itself adrift on such a journey. Only love would give itself into the hands of such a great unknown. For how shall a seed say the size of the ocean? How can a shell tell the size of the sea?

The Cities that do not Exist, exist

There are cities you come to and there are cities you will not reach, not by any road or track or mountain pathway, not by any crossing of the bridge that runs over the rush of the river, not by the ocean, not by way of valley or field or meadow.

There are cities you come to and cities that do not exist, not in the brick and mortar made from the earth by the hand of man, not in the architecture man has imagined and made, not in clay or stone or wood or metal.

No, these cities are hidden cities, without roads, cities without route of map, cities that do not know the directions, that know nothing of north and south, that do not remember the way east lies east of west and west lies west of east, know nothing of these words man has given to himself so that he may always know which direction he goes in, so that he may find his way home.

These cities you reach alone, for they are the places where your heart takes you.

The one who-is-looking-for-whom-he-loves knows many cities which are hidden from the eyes of man, knows islands that cannot be seen, knows the secret mountains, knows the valleys where he alone walks, where he walks alone. For he has followed his heart and these are the places his heart has delivered him to. He has arrived sometimes in sadness, sometimes in grief, sometimes in hope.

These cities that do not exist, exist. Their walls are as great as those of any great city. Their streets are alive with those who sing and dance and live and sleep. Their architecture is made from memories, their bricks and mortar from the tears man weeps.

Not every man will reach the same city but if they do, they do so alone. They do so without knowing how they have arrived. How long they shall stay in this city they do not know.

There are some who come to these cities and cannot leave. Their hearts may be heavy, they may not be able to cry the walls away. They do not know how many days they dwell in this city for they do not know the day, not by any name that man has given, for one day has become another. So they wander the streets, the way the days wander one into another. They do not know the names of the streets, they do not care. They do not want this city, yet it is in this city that they now abide. It is where they are.

There are some who come, and become familiar with the streets, and in time, find out where they are. They begin to see some purpose in the layout of the city, some design, some reason for it being in this place, at this time. Perhaps they discover a history they did not know, perhaps they glimpse a future they did not know. But in this they are the same as all others in the city. And having come to know all others in this place, often their lives take root here and they stay.

There are those who come and the city dissolves before their eyes as if it were never there. As if it had never existed. There are no walls. There are no roads. There is the sky, there is the earth, there is the sea, there is the day. But the day is soon over, and no matter how dark the night, it too disappears as the earth turns into the sun. Those who come to this city know how short a day is, how short a night is, how short a life is. And they travel on, for they do not need to know the routes man has supposed or laid out before them. They follow the road as it comes to them and keep their hearts open.

There are some who come and seek to leave, immediately. They cannot bear the walls, they cannot bear to be held into this city. They do not like the streets. The windows are small and let in little light. There is much noise. It is always a melancholy. So they search in the open spaces, which in the end is no different than the walls of the city if it comes from their heart. For the dark valleys can weigh as heavily on the heart as the closed door. And unless what is in their heart changes then the open spaces become the very city they seek to leave.

These are secret cities, these are hidden, invious places. What dwells in these cities depends in what dwells in your heart.

Who dwells in these cities depends on who dwells in your heart.

The City of Realisations

There is a place he knows in his heart but he cannot find. It is a city scribed into the atlas and its name is known but there is no mention of a road, no mention of the route the foot may follow, no sure way to know that one day you may arrive and finally be there.

Where is this city? He asks himself. Where is the road I do not know? And he looks around him, and it is there before him, but he does not see it because he does not notice the trees sway in the wind. He does not see the grass which lays itself down under his feet and becomes a road. He looks too far into the distance.

Where is this city? He asks of the river as it runs by, as it runs. And the river rushes and splutters and sings out to him, but the one-who-is-looking-for–whom-he-loves cannot hear what is said, for he hears only the beat of his heart and nothing else.

Where is this city? He asks of the valley, but the valley shows him nothing but where he now stands. And although the city lies in this valley, he cannot see it, because he does not want to be in the valley, because he wants to be in the city he looks for, because he wants the valley to be the way he wants it to be, not the way it is.

Where is this city? He asks of the hillside, where he climbs to the brow, where he looks far into each distance and further so that he may catch some glimpse of this city he looks for. But he cannot see it in any direction. The hillside only makes him look back at the cities he has come from.

So he looks to the darkness, and asks – where is this city? He looks to the darkness and sees only the darkness, which seems empty and void. The darkness says nothing. But the one-who-is-looking-for whom-he-loves hears only that there are no words.

Where is this city? He asks of a stranger who comes walking over the brow of the hill and through the valley by way of the river. And the stranger replies:

Ah, I see it is morning.

Mount Orison

No-one has found where this mountain ends. No-one has found where this mountain truly begins. It is a gradual climb, it deceives the senses. You are upon the path before you are aware so no-one notices the whispers of stones, or the mission of pebbles that begin this mountain, that lay the way.

It is a mountain made by all men, whether they are aware or not, whether they are aware of it or not. It rises out of the earth to reach the heavens. It is formed from clay and dust yet it is made of ether. It is seen by some, it is invisible to others, as when a mist closes over the eyes. All men give it a name and its name is heard on the lips of men the world over, even on the lips of those who do not know it is there.

Sometimes its colour is red or blue or green or yellow. Sometimes its colour is gold or silver. Sometimes it is the colour of corn, cut down. Sometimes it is the colour of eyes, crying. Sometimes the colour of someone running away, or someone returning. The colours of love, the blue mysteries, the olive tone of the shoulder, the crimsons. The colour of rain, the colour of sun. It is a colour found, when all thought it was lost.

It falls into place within the life of each man. It falls into time; an hour, a moment. It falls into the atlas of the heart, the map of the mind, the line of the heartbeat.

It is the shape of everything. Of anything. Of anyone.

But though each man gives it a name and each man gives it shape, no man knows its true size. For how shall the shell tell the size of the ocean? How shall the pebble say the sighs of the mountain? No man knows its true sighs.

Yet the mountain's sigh is the pebble.

For it is the pebble that knows the whispers of the stone, the fallen words of the clay, the eventual silence of dust. It is the pebble that rises to reach the sky, that tries to touch the heavens. It is the pebble that is upon the lips of men the world over. It is the pebble that lays the way to the mountain.

Yet no-one has found where this mountain truly begins. No-one has found where this mountain ends.

Only the one who is last upon the earth to sigh shall find himself at the end.

The City of Days

In the City of Days the pages of odysseys are written. It is here that he arrives as the miles of his journey are being described. Much has already been told, but not all, as his is a book with pages that have already been marked, with pages only partly written, with pages that lie untouched, as they have always been, waiting, waiting, waiting for the day to happen.

This is a place that before night becomes known is already aware of the stars. Everything is because of what befell the stars, everywhere is starfall, everyone has a part of the stars in their heart.

This is a place where scribes delight in all the day has told them and spend the hours of the night writing. But they must wait for the day to be over. This is a place where scribes listen to all that the night has done and spend the hours of the day in their patient art. But they must wait for the night to end.

These tomes, these books, are gathered as a man leaves, not the city, but his existence, and given over to him. Much he will have already written himself, but not all, for though the days and the nights belonged to him still there is no man who has not some small part of himself mingled into other lives. Perhaps a word, perhaps a smile. Perhaps some small gesture that he himself did not notice or attach much importance to. And perhaps that gesture was a kindness. Perhaps when he was crying he touched another's heart. They saw him wipe away his tears. He did not see them. Perhaps his hand touched against another's hand while he was walking, and they felt the warmth from him run into their heart, and their heart opened. There are many things a man does not know. There are many things a man does not see though he walks with his eyes open. There are many words a man does not hear, although he thinks he listens.

And so, it is here that he arrives, in this unfinished city. He knows it contains what has not been given over to her, what is not in the volumes of her life. Some scriptures of her love. Some pages from her book of grief. Eulogies. Deep desires. Joys. Epiphanies. Her hope. And he wants these parchments. He wants to hold them. To smell them. To read them. To touch them. To weep upon their inks. To follow their scrolls, their scrawls. To see her imaginations. He wants to find an end to this unbearable quest.

But it is not an easy task to find what you look for in this city, especially if that which you seek is not your own. For only part of her life will be written where he might find it. Only part of her life. All the other pieces are in other lives, scribbled on other parchments. In his life, in his script of love, in his words of tenderness, she will be written. So, also, will she be written into the lives of others she has touched. Into the lives of others who spoke with her, who walked with her, who watched her avoiding puddles the rain made. It would take him his monument of days to find all these separate pieces, these forgotten fragments, these memories that belong to someone else.

There are those gestures she made that she herself would have forgotten, those words she spoke that she may not have remembered, yet they still are, for they have found themselves in someone else's heart and still live, or they dwell in the invisible spheres that leave this earth and become part of the great night, and still exist.

In a life, in a short span of time, many words can be spoken and much can be done. Words as myriad as the sands on the shore, grains of a greater truth, whose hearts are moved by the sea. Destructive words, like feathers in the wind, blown this way and that way and every way. They can never be gathered, these feathers, just as the words spoken by a cruel heart can never be returned to the mouth. Joyful words that are as scattered and plentiful as the stars that fly the universe. Words of wonder and awe. Words of disappointment.

And all of these words are somewhere. Somewhere, in this city of days. Somewhere in the tombs and tomes.

But it is not an easy task, and the one-who-is-looking-for-whom-he-loves knows that his days are numbered, as are the days of all who enter this city, as are the days of all who try to avoid this city. It makes no difference to the scribes whether a man comes to them in question, or whether he walks the journey of his life without ever asking. And there are pages within books that have yet to be written. So, the one-who-is-looking-for–whom-he-loves stares a while at the city, aware of the knowledge he holds in his heart, and departs.

He sighs, and the words he says may be written into the pages of odysseys, or may lose themselves in the space of the great darkness. But he knows his words are somewhere. For though he has spoken alone, his heart remembers. And, after all, everything lies somewhere in the night.

The Tree of the Lost

It is a tree amongst trees.

In winter, when its branches are bare to the world, it is perfect. It is a perfect tree. It is a perfect tree for those who seek to find and for those who find. It is the tree of the lost. Not leaves, although each year the same seasons happen and the leaves brighten, then fade, fall, disappear, become earth. No, it is not called the Tree of the Lost because of its leaves, but because of the small things that enter a life and then leave. It could be a glove with all its red fingers, its worn out thumb, the small tear where the back of the hand lay against it. Now it is alone, its companion elsewhere. It could be an image of a dog that cannot be found, a dog whose black eyes look out at the world passing by, whose white coat is only barely seen upon the page that is pinned to the bark of the tree. For it is always something that is lost that is left upon this tree, or some token or symbol from those looking, something lost to the life it had come into, something gone.

Day by day things go missing. Day by day things are brought to this tree and attached and left hanging. Once, a card, the King of Hearts, had been left between branches. Nobody knew whether or not it was the right way up. Nobody knew whether or not it was a message between lovers, or simply a king lost to his kingdom. Nobody knew what had happened to all the other cards. Were they now useless? Once, a child's toy, broken. It was made of wood, a light wood, balsa. It sat upon wood within the woods. It was painted red and upon its one wing a yellow circle, a smiling sun. It lay unclaimed until the wind took it. But it did not go far from this tree, having lost its tail, it fell to earth. It lay there, in many small pieces, until the pieces were eventually gathered up and disposed of. Other toys, too, have been left behind, forgotten. Nobody knows their names, nor where they have come from, nor in whose life they were meant to be.

THE TREE OF THE LOST

Buttons have been found here, and keys. Buttons of all shapes and sizes, lucky and unlucky. Keys of somewhere that no-one knows. What do they open? Where do they open? Why have they been left hanging ? Why have they not been found by the one who lost them?

Scarves, humble scarves, have been tethered to these branches. Scarves striped, or feathered, woollen scarves that fight off the wind and the cold that nips your neck, silk scarves the colour of a warm day or a blue evening. Scarves with the slight scent of someone, elsewhere.

Sometimes pieces of green or red or yellow flutter from this tree. They flutter in the winds, these lost prayers, these lost wishes.

The one-who-is-looking-for-whom-he-loves comes to this tree, as he had done before. He comes with wishes, with prayers. He comes with her name upon his lips, and ties her name upon this tree, knowing there will be no answer. He knows her name will flutter in the winds, a lost name, a name that cannot be found. For three days, for nine days, for five thousand days.

For is not love greater than three days?

North of his love

Some of his nights lie to the north of his love, and whom he loves is far from where he moves and speaks and breathes. Some of his nights lie to the south of his love, to the east, to the west. It is in every direction, his love. Yet there are no miles to find it.

No matter how far he walks his love is still the same. Even if he were never to move an inch his love would be as deep, as strong. But where she has gone he does not know. How to find the miles to her he cannot say. There is no sun that will show the direction, there is no moon that will guide his footsteps along night's pathways. Even the stars say nothing.

And the shadows, in which he lies, only reveal to him that the light of his life is missing.

To the south of his love, in the sands, he had written her name. It was another ache to watch the waves come in, wash over, erase the name that had once existed. The next day he had gone to the shore again, had written her name, had watched the waves come in, wash over, erase the name that had once existed. It was another ache. No matter where he scrawled on the sand, the sea found him. And it broke his heart, the way it breaks the heart of the sands, again and again.

To the north of his love, in the snow, he had carved out her heart. He had placed her name. But the sun came, and the snow disappeared, the way her heart disappeared, and her name disappeared. Perhaps he was not far enough north of his love. But no matter how many times he carved out her heart, the sun came, the winds came, her heart was blown out of existence.

To the west he found trees, the origins, the spirits. They would hold her memory. So he spelt her name in ebony, in ash, in acajou. But other men came and cut down the trees and her name was lost among the leaves. The letters were carved and separated. And her name was no more.

He turned east, and thought to carve her name in stone. So day after day he carved, and rock let him. And when he had carved her name, he watched as the winds came, single-threaded, and then disappeared. And rock held her name. He watched as the sun came into the sky and was mighty, and watched as the gold fell down into the sea. And rock held her name. One day, other men said, it will be erased. Nothing lasts forever.

Yes, his love was in every direction. Yet there are no miles to find it.

A road through a valley in darkness

He had seen darkness before, but only that of the night when the stars still shone and the moon was over the valley, and the light that man had made out of the earth was everywhere. In this place he now stands, still, alone, still alone, is the true darkness, the darkness that was before man ever began, that was before man made light. The darkness is such that you cannot see the shape of the night. The darkness makes all colours become one, all shapes become one, and every line and thread and curve arched into this darkness become one. And here, in this valley in darkness, of the stars and the moon there is nothing at all.

It is a place of fear, a place of dread. It is a place where someone can stand before you and you cannot see them. You cannot feel their existence. There is no way to know they are there for even if a word falls from their mouth and they cry out to you, your heartbeat is in your ears so you cannot hear them. And, should they rise above the beat of your heart, should their words come to you, you cannot say whether it is miles or inches to them, you cannot say whether it is north or south. You cannot say if it is any direction at all. Wordfall becomes heartbeat, so you don't know if you have heard anything from anywhere.

The darkness has made him fear everything. Each slow step, each breath, each second. He cannot find the hollows of footprints. He cannot adjust his senses to this darkness. His hands reach out into an empty space. He cannot tell if he is at the edge of everything or in the middle of nowhere. He cannot tell if his next step is in air, on earth, in water. He smells nothing, no-one. Where once the way was familiar and sure, now the same steps are unsteady, uncertain. In his desperation and confusion he cries out into the darkness, but only the sound of a heartbeat is heard.

A ROAD THROUGH A VALLEY IN DARKNESS

Time has lengthened itself out, stretched itself everywhere.

Space, in its endlessness, has closed in. His foot travels more slowly than it has ever done before yet there is nowhere to go and no way of knowing where to go.

But it is the aloneness in which he is, alone in the darkness of a valley without moon, without stars, without even a flame, a glimmer, a glance of light, an ember. It is a valley in pure darkness, a darkness that was before he ever began.

The Islands that are not of this world

He had heard many things. He had been told many places to go. He had been told places he must see. Places he should see. Places that would end his quest. Places where his journey would be over. Places that those who told him, though they had not seen these places themselves, knew existed. They were islands far to the east. There were lands far to the west. In the far north lay places of great happiness. In the far south lay the sand, the sea, and pure contentment. Gardens were described, and islands. Places of great majesty. Places of repose. Places were age does not matter, and one's heart is always in the full bloom of youth. Places were only joy was experienced, yet everything was understood. These places were like nothing he had ever seen on his journeys. Yes, he had been told many places to go and had been given many directions. Even to reach one of these places there were a hundred different routes. Do all roads lead to this place? But these places were not on the map of his heart, so he did not know them.

He was confused. Each man seemed adamant in his descriptions, in his directions. Each seemed adamant that he alone was right, and that the others were wrong, or had been mislead, or had left the path, or did not truly know the way. Each seemed adamant that this place he had described was true, existed, and that the others were a mirage, a fata morgana, an illusion, a deceit. Yet who was he to believe?

The ways were varied, yet the places seemed much the same. He had heard whisperings of these places before, but now, in his loss, words flowed like a torrent from the tongues of others, who did not know his loss. How could they know, for the loss was far in the abyss of his heart and scaled the mountains of his mind, and encompassed everything.

He could bear no more talk. He could bear no more confusion. He left this place where no-one listened, and went into his own solitude. He knew that whatever was written in his heart, he would find. Wherever his heart told him to go, he would go. And he knew he must listen to his heart, for it was here that his journeys were chosen. And it was here that his quest would end. For he held in his heart a place of hope and, above all, he held in his heart a place of love.

For there are places not of this earth and they are impossible to find if they are not written into your heart.

A city of silver

He is set adrift, this man, the one-who-is-looking-for-whom-he-loves. There is no course, there is no portolan, no harbour, no distance to achieve, no destination to arrive at. It is as if he has given himself over to the sea and his heart beats to the rhythm of both ebb and flow, as if he has let go of the earth he once stood upon, and lets himself be taken wherever he is taken and he floats and looks at the sun. He drifts and is mesmerized by moonlight. There is a stillness in his heart. He does not know time. He cannot tell you how long he has been drifting.

He no longer searches, he no longer questions, and his journey drifts him onto the shore of an island, and he arises out of the sea and stands and looks around him. It is night, and he sees moonlight. The sands are silver. The distant city on the height is silver. It is a city that looks at the moon. It is a city surrounded by stars. They fall onto the shoulders of the city and hide its heart. All that can be seen are the great silver walls and a cloud of starlight. It is a city he does not remember, yet deep within him he feels he knows this city, as if it had once been a part of him.

He feels as if he can see the streets of the city, as if he is in them, walking. He feels as if he stands alone on a height against the night, watching the stars, listening to the distant sound of a river winding its way to the sea. He feels he stands within great walls which are of silver in the night, but which are of gold in the day. What is he looking for? Above him are stars. But there are stars in every part of this very city he imagines himself to be in. Look, the names of stars are on each road, star signs upon the tops of buildings, on their doors, on their walls. An atlas of other parts of night. And he looks at these things yet he thinks only of her. Because, once, he had brought her the stars.

He had found them in the shapes man had devised, in circular metals, in names, in scripts. He had found them in a shape that can be held in the hand. He had found this and he had brought it to her and told her the stars. And it was real, this instrument that spoke of stars. It was real. It lay in her room of books. Where she had left it, before she was lost.

And now he is lost. And he wants to leave this island of silence with its city of silver. Its city of stars. For it is an empty place, more lonely than a solitude. He can find no-one. It is as if everyone has been forgotten, though the great city still stands. As if it belonged to some other time, or some other place, or some other heart. And he no longer knows whether this city is his own memory or dream, or if it is the memory or dream of some other.

It may be this island, these walls of silver, are no more than a page in a Book of Days in a City of Days. It may be this part of his heart belongs to some other. There are many enigmas in the night, and the one-who-is-looking-for-whom-he-loves knows this. One answer is given him and another question opens.

As he stands on the shore he opens his heart and listens to the song of the night. It is a song that can be heard across the island, and even out into the sea. It is carried on the winds. It echoes through the valley. But it is a song of both beginning and ending. And as night sings, it brings a longing into his heart for something he cannot have, for something he cannot quite remember, he does not know, yet he knows more than his own heartbeat. It is a quest for something that is lost.

And the night sings, but he does not know why.

The way of the Eremite

And in wandering he came to the beginning. It was a pathway, roughly hacked from tall bushes that struggled on their way to fulfillment, clusters of grasses that would not give up, trees determined to hide what was beyond them. But there was little left of the leaves, for it was autumn. And what had been was turned to gold, and what was was tempered into bronze and shaped for the falling. So much was revealed to the one-who-is-looking-for-whom-he-loves. There were scattered shadows, for the sun was divided through the trees. It was early morning.

This was an unknown path, one he had not travelled before. It was not on the map written by his heart, it was not on any atlas he had seen. It was nowhere he knew of. So he put his foot upon this path. And his journey began with this first step. The rock was hard under the sole of his foot, and it supported him in his climb, for it was steady. The grasses brushed against him, and the dew sparkling in those thin blades came trickling onto his feet like tears and washed him. He pushed against twigs and branches, and the thorns that caught his hand drew blood. He was not deterred. He had been through a valley in darkness, and his heart was already heavy. He was not afraid of the shadows, for he could see the light. And before him he could also see the curve of the way he followed, so he knew there was a further mystery.

Turning into the woodland he scarcely found a path, there was only the disturbance of leaves to show the way. So he followed the feuillemort, followed the signs left behind by whomever was here. But it did not take long for him to discover who it was. Having walked a distance of heartbeats he came across a man, who sat, as if waiting for him.

Without introduction the man beckoned him to sit. So he sat

among the leaves, and rested his back against the strength of stone, and listened.

He looked into the eyes of the man who spoke. He could not decide whether those eyes were as blue as a sky falling into the ocean, or as earth-speckled as these leaves, this autumn, or as deep as darkness. He could not decipher whether the eyes of this man were watching some other world, or watching him alone. He could not decide whether he knew these eyes as some part of his heart, or whether this man was truly a stranger unto him. But he saw compassion in these eyes, and understanding. And the one-who-is-looking-for-whom-he-loves began to cry.

Now he could not see through his own tears. The colours of autumn were lost, and the dappled sunlight played with the shadows and would not stop, so that nothing was clear to him now. He could no longer see the eyes of the man, but he could hear his voice. And it was the voice of the winds when they whisper to you that which you need to know, and it was the voice inside the heart, the one you always listen to, and it was the sound of the sea soothing him, lulling him into repose. It was deep and warm. And the one-who-is-looking-for-whom-he-loves lay down, and placed himself upon the earth, and buried his face in the leaves and sobbed.

There was no clock to tell the hours he had been there. But the sun had moved in the sky and the shadows had fallen in another direction. The man with compassion in his eyes had gone, moved on, had walked away to wherever he had walked to. But he had left words in the wind that whispered and he had left words within the heart that could not be erased.

Even though he was in the woods, the one-who-is-looking-for-whom-he-loves could hear the sea, could see the sky falling into the ocean, could once again see the colours of the leaves of autumn, earth-speckled. But it was different now, not just because of the sun and the shadows falling other directions, but because of his heart, which for a while had been sheltered, which for a while had been understood.

And as he lay awhile and remembered, the deep voice of the stranger came out of his heart and he heard the words he had spoken.

"In time beyond us, what is this time between you? It is but a space, a breath. It is but a moment...".

The Valley where the moon is caught in the trees

In the Valley where the moon is caught in the trees and cannot find her love, she has broken her heart into a thousand pieces and given them to the river that the river might carry her heart into a thousand different places and she might find her love.

In the Valley where the moon is caught in the trees the sylvan warriors hold back her claim. Like sentries with myriad hands, they will not let her pass. They will not let her find her love. They are like the hundred-handed ones, who fought so hard against the darkness. Like Argos, yet without eyes. Night after night she falls upon them. Night after night they hold her there in the sky. Night after night she cries to the river. Night after night the river does not reply.

For the trees are afraid, and the river is afraid. They have heard that the moon can pull the heartstrings of the sea, of the ocean, and move them. They do not know what will happen if the moon leaves the sky to be with her love, and lies slumbering, and does not follow the course of the heavens. They do not know what will happen if she lets go the heartstrings of the sea, if she leaves the darkness without her solitary brightness.

So in fear the trees armour themselves and will not sleep. So in fear the river rushes away from the moon and hides in dark places where the fragments of the selenian heart, the slivers, lose themselves and disappear.

And so the man-who-is-looking-for-whom-he-loves looks at the moon. He watches the trees. He listens to the rush of the river as it hurries by.

He feels he is the moon, caught in the trees, crying to the river. And he knows that if he could find his love he too would leave the darkness.

Water shows the hidden heart

Travelling east, past the central, settled plains until he can almost taste the flavour of the sea, he comes to a place nestled amongst high hills. These hills have rolled over and back again in their sleep and remain slumbering. Amongst them an old volcanic peak holds itself up, bare to the world, and puts its head in the clouds. It too remains slumbering. It does not speak. At its feet what is left of the woodland stretches out over the hills, into the glens and further, into the pockets of the landscape, the valleys. There is a rich currency of leaves in this garden and the grass never ceases to be.

It is here he comes to lay down his burden, for a while. It is here he comes to notice the sky. It is a canvas painted by the patience of blue. Here and there it moves, and moves again. But these clouds do not remember him, and pass by without so much as a tear in their eyes.

It is here he comes to appreciate the trees, all of them, in all their colours. The evergreens, the sturdy sons, the good sons, stay and watch and remember the way they have done through every season. Their wealth is their constancy. They are strong enough in themselves to know glory does not matter. They cherish their green leaves. They have lost nothing since the last time he was here, but have grown into the world. But the prodigals are in their pride, displaying their riches of gold, showing off to the world. They clothe themselves in crimsons, in bronze, and in the most amazing yellows. They cannot stop this frenzy. They know they are admired and so they squander their inheritance. But soon they will lose these riches. Soon all will be lost. It is already foretold. Everyone knows it to be so.

It is here he comes to reflect on the waters that have gathered in this place over the seasons. They have studied the world, they have accepted the sky. Clouds come and go in their presence. The sun cannot resist their freedoms, and follows them from their beginnings and flows with them to their end. But it is not their end, it is merely another beginning. It is a place they did not know, another existence. Having been conceived by the sky, having been born amongst rock, out of the great stone of the earth, having fallen through both sky and earth, they arrive at the great openness of the sea, and are absorbed, and become one with the sea, the great body of water.

But in this place they, too, pause a while and reflect on themselves. He looks into the eyes of the water and sees the sky. He sees its permanence, he sees its ephemeral nature. He looks into the eyes of the water and sees the hylean gods, the sylvan spirits. He sees the length of the life of a leaf. He sees abundance and emptiness. He looks into the eyes of the water and sees his own eyes, looking. They reflect everything, these waters, even the hidden heart.

It is here he comes to feel the breath of the wind. It has always been gentle in this place. It does not disturb the trees, yet the leaves fly in full chorus. It is playful with grasses. It combs the hair of the water that lies gathered in pools. It whispers to flora. They are like lovers in the long grass and all that the wind whispers to her is her secret. It is flora's secret, what is said.

And what the winds say to him he already knows in his heart.

Endlong into midnight

The-one-who-is-looking-for-whom-he-loves stands as the day is leaving and watches the evening fall in and the even-star rise. Never does the day say goodbye, it simply goes, sometimes stealing away when he is not looking, sometimes surprising him with its sudden departure. Already indigo, the sky begins to reveal its deeper desires and opens its heart so that all may see the perfect darkness which was before they ever began. Hues of indigo give way to the ebony eyes of night, and the sky paints itself with stars.

From where he is, the man who is so small in the size of the universe, listens to his heart beat and looks into the darkness. He sits upon rock, rock jutting out of the earth, rock reaching up out of the shadows. Upon this jut-jaw of land he rests, and simply observes, and lets the night do whatever it does. He feels the wind touch his face, and thinks of whom he loves. He hears the sough of the wind in the trees. He hears the leaves quivering.

Beyond the trees, where the village lives, a thousand little lights. Beyond the trees, where the ocean resides, a swell of darkness. Beyond the trees, a clock that does not mention the day, does not know the night, cares nothing for the hour. Hands closed over itself, it does not stir. There is no heartbeat. Once in the day it tells the truth. Once in the night it announces to the world what should be known. But no-one notices. So used are they to the hands standing still, to the movement of time that is not there, they give no glance towards the small tower anymore. For they know there is nothing written on its face. They know it has nothing to say.

In other places there are clocks that will not stop. They insist on your knowing. They insist that all who see them know the moment they are losing, and every moment they are losing, and all that is lost. So many freedoms disappear this way.

In other places where the ocean resides, it comes and goes between darkness and light. Here, too, beyond the trees, the sea journeys between the course the moon takes and the path of the god of light. It bathes the moon, it shows the god how great is the light of the day. It comes and goes.

In other places villages live, and their lights appear in the evening as small constellations, as if they echo some part of the sky, of the night, as if they speak to the universe, to whatever there is.

Endlong into midnight the one-who-is-looking-for-whom-he-loves listens to his heart beat and looks into the darkness.

They are many more stars than he had imagined. And he begins to do what all men do when they stare into the night, he follows the stars. He follows their form, their tracery, their pattern. He follows the shape he imagines them to make. He knows it is his own fallacy, he knows it is his own way of marking the heavens. He follows them to find himself, to know his way home when there is no other to guide him. He follows them so he will not feel alone and helpless, a smallness in the greatness, a heartbeat in an age he cannot count. A being brought forth in the unimaginable, from the unimaginable. A being brought forth from an earth which is less than a pearl in the darkness.

And he feels he shall fall off this earth. And he feels the earth is falling. Falling through oceans of darknesses, falling far from the place it once was, far from where it has been and cannot be again, and he prays some hand will retrieve this earth, will save it, will cherish it.

His head is light. His body lies down upon the earth. His hands reach out to touch clay. Lying with his back to the great wall of the earth he feels his heartstrings stretched to their very limit, taut, like the string of the bow of the Loxian; the archer god, the god of light, of prophecy, of truth. But what truth? What prophecy, what god?

And the man, lying alone in the universe, feels the wind move through his fingers, hears the wind breathing, moving the waves upon the ocean. Feels his clothes move in the wind, feels his hair move in the wind. Watches the wind move the trees, watches the wind move the leaves.

And the one-who-is-looking-for-whom-he-loves considers this. Among so many questions, a question: Who moves my heart?

The parable of day

Descending the hill, much fell from his view. Before, there was valley, dappled townships, rooftops, treetops, the green swathe of the new-born fields, the run of hedgerows that bordered and shepherded grass. Before, there was the sea and the harbour that would not let go of the sea and the boats that tried to flee from the sea. Now, with each turn, a hylean world towered into the sky.

The bent larch, long-blown by winds from the one direction, leans over as if to listen to the words men say. It tells them nothing but the winds of other seasons. Beyond it, the tall pines are stationed together like soldiers, stand as if always on duty, say nothing, show their strength. Close by, the sweet chestnuts, ladies of leisure, with their bejewelled fingers and the way they lay back into the world under their parasols. The sycamores ply their wares. Merchants that do not move, except in autumn, when they let go all their riches. And there is ash, as always. Holly is here, and ivy that climbs into the heart of the king of the woods, and is not afraid. Together they crowd the sky and so the one-who-is-looking-for-whom-he-loves did not resist their view of the world, but wandered, as freely as the wind wanders through the trees, and walked until he could walk no more.

Charcoal had made a small circle in the earth. Ashes told the tale of a man. So he was here, thought the one-who-is-looking-for-whom-he-loves, he is near, close by. For the fire was still smouldering and the embers were only now falling into themselves. The eremite was here.

So he waited for the hermit to return to this place. He sat by the embers, and put his back against the strength of stone, and rested. He looked at the woods, he remembered the trees, but the leaves were a different colour. The pathways had not been wept upon. The stones that were lost in the woods were still lost in the woods. Much was as it was, but not all. For that is the way of the world. Everything eventually changes, all things pass.

Then there was the slow return of the hermit. Slow, like the passing of the sun through the hours on a summer's day, when there is no hurry towards night. In winter the day cannot wait, but all through the length of the season it takes it's time and saunters into the evening. Slow, like the scent of verbena as it finds its way to you through the air and lingers as if it can't decide where to go, what to do.

When the hermit returned he said nothing. It was dark now. He sat down and began another fire. Out of the embers a phoenix of flame. It was one small fire amongst the many fires of the night. And then he lay down and looked at the sky.

He pointed to a star. A small star you could barely see, a star far in the distance. You almost had to close your eyes to know it was there. So the one-who-is-looking-for-whom-he-loves lay down and looked at the star. He almost closed his eyes, almost. And as he peered into the darkness he heard the voice of the eremite say:

Night is the parable of day.

For when the earth turns into the night, away from the day, away from the light and looks at what is always there, it asks itself:

How shall the star say the size of the universe? How shall the shell tell the sighs of the sea?

The Room of Books

This is a place he knows well. If she is not here, she is nowhere. This is the room of books. Her room. Her books. Running fingers along spines, following the letters that follow themselves up and down and around, smelling the scent of paper, of ink, of imagination, knowing she has touched each one. And then he stops. Stops moving. Stops and stands still. For no reason. The strength of a spine accepts his fingers, and he pulls a book down from the shelf and turns the title towards him. Upon the spine, her name. Upon the shoulders of the book, upon that which carries everything within, one word. Amarantine. He opens it. He opens this book. He opens it and inside, on these pages, is the story of her love, and his eyes rush along the lines of words with which she describes him. In the first page she has written to him an inscription which reads :

"Out of your heart came woods of beautiful name and countries to dream of…"

He knew well what was spoken of. He knew well, and his heart missed a beat. "woods of beautiful name" "countries to dream of…" and then one word. Her name.

Beyond this page lies love.

Mile upon mile of her expression.

Every inch.

He begins to read:

Amarantine

for
Nicholas

Amarantine

You know when you give your love away
it opens your heart,
everything is new.
And you know time will always find a way
to let your heart believe it's true.

You know love is everything you say;
a whisper, a word,
promises you give.
You feel it in the heartbeat of the day.
You know this is the way love is.

Amarantine… amarantine…amarantine…
love is…love is….love…

You know love may sometimes make you cry,
so let the tears go,
they will flow away,
For you know love will always let you fly
-how far a heart can fly away!

Amarantine…amarantine…amarantine…
love is…love is…love…

You know when love's shining in your eyes
it may be the stars
fallen from above.
And you know love is with you when you rise,
for night and day belong to love.

The psalm of little things

There is no simple song to love.
It is full of everything.

It is the psalm of little things;
the touch, the word, the look.

It is the ode of exaltation,
it is the lament, it is the despair.

It is filled with every grief.
It is a sadness sung from nowhere.

It is the hymn of hope,
it is for him, it is for her.

It is the air that each one breathes,
it is centre, edge, beginning, end.

It is everything our small hearts need.
It is the rise and fall of all who ever loved, and then

it is more than diamond, ruby, pearl,
it is more than a rule, a place, a prayer.

It is the song that is sung
full of everything, everywhere.

I stitch your wounds

Nobody knows how much you love me.

You armour our love against the world.
I stitch your wounds.

You know the years our love has travelled.
I place milestones along the inches.

You say there is no last season to our love
so I lay out winter as another beginning.

You declare our love openly in gesture, in word.
I remember all the secret moments.

You say to the world how much you love me.
In each heartbeat all of my love is given.

Nobody knows how much I love you.

indigo for night

scattered with silver

vermilion for mouth of lips and edgings

dark green silk
for what comes over and above
her incarnadine curves and deeper hollows

crimson for where there is no other colour

red
for each effort of love
each furnace each passion

white
for the marks that show against his shoulder

the amethyst purples
for what the mind makes
and imagines

darkness for eyes and brightness

black
for the strands that lie against a snow of pillow
that cannot keep themselves from falling

and gold
touched by gold becomes gold

gold that is no more than any other colour

for all colours say themselves in love

Pilgrim stone

Her mouth was a pilgrim stone on the way to love.

He travelled her lips
until he came
to the place
where they settled themselves into him.

The way they fell,
the way they closed upon him,
was carved forever in his heart.

He followed faithfully.
He was a pilgrim
going to the place of his desire,
to that one place - love.

Along the trail,
across the tiny lines of her intensity,
he was tireless
for knowledge.

Until he had travelled her lips
he had been a blind man, searching.

A poor man, pleading.
A beggar, reaching out.

Now, at this place of worship,
he was given eyes.

It's true

His voice is sung warm;
it winds through the air
the colour of sun on a glorious day.

But it is more than this.

It is the sensual midnight, the curious moon, the lost lover.
It is the voice in the cloudless blue
and the fallen yellows of autumn finding their way.

It is the stones in the woods and the leaves in the forests.
It is riverrush, it is morningrise, it is day.

It is the letters he carved so you would remember his promise.
It's true! It's true!

It is a moment wanting to live forever.

It is more than the sun, his voice.
It is more than a sky of blue.

It is the soft replying of his love to you.

The eyes had let go secrets

It was already tangible
and yet nothing had been said.
But the eyes had let go secrets,
and the hands had laid down battle plans
in the conquest of love.

Arrows, was it?
Love-tipped. Love-struck. God-shot.
Or was it simply his eyes, shining?

Divine Archery?
Or was it simply that his words
flew into her mouth and conquered?

A flaming sword, a captive moment,
a daring deed, a magic potion,
a knight in armour? Or, arrows, was it?

She knew nothing of these as love slew her heart.
It was his eyes, shining.

the temple of moments

there was a sadness
looking out of his eyes
as if
longwritten into the temple of moments
there had arisen
a grief
he could not speak of

and there
within
amassing in silence
all the sad journeys of secrets

what it was
or
why it was
he did not know

he could not find
in the inks of ancient pages
or the leaves
that tell you the name of the day
any trace
of that world of shadows

so all the words he should have said
were in his heart;

unsalvaged

his breath was like the wind
blown backwards;
an utterance that could not happen

for the winds
kept whatever they had gathered;
his savage pulse
that persistent rhythm
all that had happened

- the chasm

I sing you my love

I sing you my love
I sing you my passion

I sing you my love
but you hear only sadness
and it makes your cry

I sing you my love
but it is sharp
and anything that pierces your heart
cannot be forgiven

I sing you my love
but you will not hear me
and leave love hanging in the air
alone and striving

I sing you my love
but the sound of my words hurt you
they are the sound of your pain
though your pain is silent

I sing you my love
I sing you my passion

I sing you my love
but you do not hear me
and my song is lost in the day

am I without deliverance?

sagas and longtales

So many words he said with his eyes.
So many words no-one knew had ever existed.

Out of those darknesses the eulogy of endless desire.
Out of those softnesses sagas and longtales.

Out of earth colours, an odyssey of islands.

Out of pinpoints of light, valleys and cities, exquisitely described.
Everything he could imagine was in his eyes.

Even if it never reaches the kiss

is already done.

With the thought.
With the glance.
With the sigh.

Even if it never reaches the kiss.

Even if it means
you never find each other in the touch.
It is already done.

It is enough.

Here

Here
>is where he found his love
and here
>love came without name

here
>is where his heart shone out
and here
>his eyes beheld moonlight

Here
>is here he gave everything to love
and here
>love gave him everything

He was not afraid

To resist him
she armed herself
with coldness,
with the very chill a winter weaves
for its journey onward.

To confront him
she shivered her voice,
she frosted her bones.

To confuse him
she had frozen her stare
so he could not fathom her,
so he would not dare.

To defeat him
she clothed herself in ice.

"His heart cannot conquer me now"
she said to her soul,
knowing it was not so;
she told her heart,
but it was already
burning from desire,
erupting into flowing inches of love
everywhere.

Still, she fought.

Her words were sharp.
His were soft and yielding.

Her hands were hard.
His held tenderness and warmth.

Her mouth rampaged.
His mouth tempered all her forces.

Her eyes would not give anything way,
would not betray, would not let anything be told.
His eyes were strong. His eyes were steady. His eyes were bold.

He had a secret she did not know.
He was not afraid of the cold.

Whispered myths

Everything he said he wrapped around her

Words were heard
in the space between their lips

Forever he said
as she closed her eyes into love

You she sighed
giving him every treasure

No-one knew the myths he whispered to her
No-one knew her fabledoms
They alone knew these things

The smallest whisper

She closed her eyes.

Wind scripts.
Pilgrim sighs.

Sometimes
he was no more than a spider's walk
across her skin,
a warmness weaving, a soft wind.

In this way love was woven over her.

His breathing, his breath,
the smallest whisper,
the echo of his heart.

He adored her hair.
He idolised the waves.
Made secrets from the strands.

They fell apart.

He had unravelled her.
Erratic hands.
Orectic mouth.

His tongue was fire.
His lips were echoes of the same.
His fingers were fine rain.

At the nape, any defense she had, failed.

She could not explain

It was already said.

Still she insisted on his sonorous promises,
not for their words,
but for the deep root of his voice
which echoed into her, declaring all of itself.

There was nothing of her
that it did not seek out and devour.

No inch unnoticed.
No thread unmentioned.
He tangled everything
so that when her heart pulled apart
it stretched into an endlessness she could not explain.

"You are the flame by which my heart shall perish"
he had said to her,
not knowing
it was by his own flame
that her love was forged and her heart had melted into embers.

It was their own

Some words she said only in love.
Some gestures she made were only for him.

It was alone among them,
the love that knew no-one else in the world.

It was their own and it was wonderful.

Her heart knew more of him than any other ever could
and he knew everything in her eyes.

Nothing could hide from the years of knowing
or from love.

It was their own and it was wonderful.

not spoken of..

First
the empty space between them

Then
that which was filled with their words
with their lips
with their hands

Fingers fell
Words disappeared
Lips became kiss

More than this is not spoken of..

He reads until he can read no more. There are more words but he cannot see them, he cannot say them, for his eyes have a mist before them and his mouth can only utter her name. He lets his fingers fall through her words until they reach the end. The last pages are empty. It is as if she still had love to write but it is not written. He finds himself weeping. Her hands have been on this book, her heart is in it. She is scattered in these pages.

He sinks slowly to the floor, he has fallen into the abyss. Here, there is no dreaming. Here, there is no hope. And so he weeps tears as if he were the sky, crying. And his tears fall and fall and fall upon a book that lies looking up at him, accepting his tears. It is as if the book were gathering his tears into its own heart. And he stares at the book and reaches out to it. The cover is hard, as if made to last. Strong, like metal. Almost silver, like the moon. Through his tears he can see words written on the cover: The book of Grief.

He wonders whether he should open it, as he can bear no more sadnesses. But he knows it is her book, so he looks.

There are no words in it. For who can describe sadness and grief? It is not a book whose pages are bound, for grief cannot be bound. It is a box filled with tear-stained pages. Each one. Tear-stained. It is as if the colours of the earth had wept through her eyes. Some had cried for one thing alone, some had cried for everything, everywhere. Some had cried viridian, vermilion, violet. Umbers, burnt and raw. Sienna. Some had cried black, to protect, when she had wanted to harbour herself, when she had wanted to surround herself and hide in the darkness. Some are colours that once were, but have fled, so that there is only a scarmark upon the page. The purples had fallen when her soul wept. Red, when her heart was on fire. Some had cried crimson over her lips and out of her mouth. Some had cried no colour at all. But were these tears her tears alone, or was there a world wept into this book? For it was as if the sky had never ceased crying and all its tears were here, in these pages. Tears that held each colour of the sky, tears like rain,

rain that brought the melancholy of a lost summer and rain that sparkled like the eyes of a woman in love. And his own tears fall into this book, are given to these pages. For these pages are the pages of a book of grief, unbound. And he closes this book of grief that cannot be bound, this box of tears.

Buried beneath grief, books. Buried beneath books, a book. Its cloth is plain white. Its size is enough, although the title of the book has melted into the whiteness, and only the indentation tells him its name:

The Atlas of wherever you are.

He opens this strange book and finds himself. He finds himself looking at everywhere he has travelled, looking for her. Each turn of a page reveals a place he has been. Here, the Isle of Revenants. There, a City of Words of blue and yellow and green and red. The atlas of where I have been, he allows himself to muse, until he turns to the next page.

He finds himself on this penultimate page. He finds himself almost at the end. Stunned, he reads the title: The Room of Books. It is where he is, at this moment. It is this room, this same room he stands in now looks at him from the pages of this book. It shows him a book. It is the Book of Winds, but it is closed, so he does know what lies within it. It shows him the book, but not where it is. It shows him a book he has not yet found, not yet seen, is only now aware of. Yet it must be somewhere in this room. He cannot now resist fulfilling the prophecy of what he sees before him, and begins to search frantically through the library of books, the forest of pages. Doors are flung open and volumes cast aside. The books are in chaos. The names of fungi cover Herodotus. Labyrinths fall open and lie above words in commotion. The Gods of greek rivers mingle with runes. Crow is now creased and the words confuse themselves.

An atlas opens its strong arms and lets loose all its separate kingdoms. Everywhere falls through the air; places he did not know, places he knew, mountains that meant nothing to him, islands he glimpsed as they were swallowed and submerged, countries to dream of, woods of beautiful name, oceans that describe themselves and seas that say their colours, rivers with nowhere to go and nothing to say, a city where the name of a woman rises, names that tempt his eyes but flee too quickly, so that his hands cannot recover them. Every shape given name. Every shape falling.

Familiar Wild Flowers now reveals snowdrops and snowflakes. Now reveals the creeping thistle. Now reveals the meadow saffron. Now turning their eyes to the world small words emerge and look into the light. In its companions the wild violets are hidden in their tomb of paper and the butterfly orchis is buried in words of moist woodland; its morning scent lost, its evening aroma no longer given over to others. The burdock remains unseen. Another book tells him of paper sailors and trumpet shells as it glides before his eyes and falls, falls and turns over, turns over and then stays, telling the world of stone piercers.

A large book tumbles down, brown in its speckledness. He can smell the age of the pages. He can see the words that trouble sleep and his eyes catch a glimpse of waves. He can see the name of a woman whose words utter into the air and are lost. He does not have time to know her truth, before he can read her words, they are gone.

There are manuscripts here also, large pages, notes written on parchment which sing.

There are images of light finding their way into the air and finding themselves some further place. And her eyes are smiling out of them.

But nothing of the Book of Winds. Does this book exist? He cannot find it A book of winds, winds? Stories, descriptions, features, terminologies, what? Still he tears books from their places, studies their titles, discards them.

He looks again at the Atlas of where he is to see if it can tell him anything more, and finds that although he sees a book of winds, it is a different book. It is a different wind. The first book he saw was the colour of snow edged by indigo. The wind itself lay down under the midnight, but was not sleeping. He had expected fury with this wind, yet all he could see where the eyes of a woman in love. This book that now looks at him is a wind the colour of a blue evening, when the stars are dreaming of the sky, and nothing is quite ready, yet everything is almost there.

Maybe he did not read the titles correctly and has already had his hands upon this book only to lose it?

Maybe.

Maybe not.

Maybe it is the next book he will turn over. Maybe it is not in this room. Maybe she was reading it elsewhere, somewhere outside, somewhere among the broken faces of granite, where she loved to go, and at the height of the broken stone, stand against the wind. No, maybe not. Keep looking. Keep looking. He glances again at the Room of Books and again the Book of Winds has changed. It is the south wind who moves through this room now. It is the south wind which opens its mouth and if it were about to say...

In his frenzy he stumbles over books he has cast to the floor. Fallen, he pulls himself to his knees, and sits for a moment, gathering his thoughts, catching his breath. So often he had seen her sitting on this same floor, in this same place, writing. How often he had come to this room to speak with her, and she would look up and smile and her eyes would betray her love. And then it dawned on him.

The stack of books he had not noticed before. They stood one upon another as some island the rain could have cried, they stood in an ocean of carpet. They all lay open, their secrets exposed. They came from everywhere, spoke about everything, gathered together in debate, but they had one thing in common. Her. She was reading these, he remembered, she was reading these books before she was lost. Before he lost her.

Slowly he lifts each book. The first to come into his hands is a book the colour of autumn. Upon it is written The Keeper of Leaves. He opens it to find no script, no words, only leaf after leaf of leaves. A collection of myriad leaves. Leaves made from water and colour on leaves made from wood and rag. They are paintings, impressions, colours, patterns. The leaves are not ordered, not classified, not filed under any system. They bear no name. It seems as if they are, and that is enough. There is no explanation as to why they are arranged, or if they are arranged, but they are in her hand, she had held that brush, she had placed something of herself upon these pages. These are something of herself, that is enough.

It is then that he comes across The Odyssey. He knows this book. She had spoken of it many times. She would tell him tales from this book. He could hear her voice in these words, it was like the voice of Scheherazade in its enchantment, in its excitement, in its amazement. Her voice would never fade from the heart of one who listened to her. She would tell him stories of the islands as they would lie and look at the stars. She would tell him of the great journey, and she would ponder how each man has his own odyssey.

And she would say to him how thankful she was to life, to fortune, to fate, to god, to chance, that she had been able to sail on her great journey with one man, with him. He remembered this. He remembered this. He remembered, too, that her favourite tale amongst these tales was that of the island of the keeper of winds, the king of the winds, Aeolus, the earth-destroyer, the many coloured. The keeper whose name was moving and changeable. The island he lived upon was a floating island, which was apt, as this island was not found in the same place twice. This island is like the earth, she would say. In our knowledge of the universe, this island earth has never been in the same place twice, not since its birth has it occupied the same space of space. It is forever in motion for the earth does not stand still, no matter what they say. It is like the island of the winds.

It moves.

So he opens the book at the where Odysseus encounters the keeper of the winds. He hurries through words, through phrases, through paragraphs, but there is nothing. He finds only the tale of a man, a sailor of the sea, a king who had been ten years fighting, one known for cleverness, strength, trickery. A madman who was not mad. A nobody. He finds only the tale of the keeper of the winds, the one who held the great breaths of the day so they could not destroy the earth. The one who seemed so content in his walls of bronze. The one who did not die and fall into the darkness, but who still dwells in the cave of the winds. He finds only a tale of the winds, the children of the god of night, the children of the goddess of morning, the dawn. He lays down this odyssey. But his own odyssey has not ended. He does not find what he seeks, he does not know what he is looking for.

His hands fall upon a set of three books. They are usually sit one beside the other, they usually lie with the strong arms of a slipcase around them; it was meant to protect them. But in this island of books, they lie open, as all others do. He takes one of the companions into his hands. The pages of this first book are bound in a deep blue. There is a portrait etched into its cover. It has the name of a country upon its hands, a country to dream of... It is not what he supposes it to be. The second book is a black book with a portrait etched into its cover. It has eyes of ebony. It has the name of a beautiful wood upon its chest, yet inside there is a history of light on paper. The third book is in red. It has the name of a city upon its shoulder, yet the face of a woman. A woman in love, whose eyes sparkle like the rain. He spends a long time with these books, these books with the names of a city, a country, a wood. These books the deepness of blue, the darkness of black, the passion of red. They are of his heart, these books.

From his reverie, from his small moments of repose, back into his angst. He leaves down these histories and his odyssey begins to write once more into his book of days.

So he looks beyond these books. He looks at a strange book, looking at him; arms open, eyes open, heart open. In this tome a strange script, a strange hand. Words he does not know lie across these pages. They are faint images, as if impressions of another page, as if merely a shadow of what should have been said.

As he follows the book page by page, he comes across her writing in the margins. She has scribbled notes, translations, ideas. He looks at the unfamiliar script and then he looks at her words. And suddenly he is aware. The City of Solitudes, she has scribbled beside marks. Marks that stand alone on a page. Symbols, emblems, cipheric script. He turns the pages more quickly now to find if there is any other thing she has written. Yes, here it is again. On a page, where words stand alone, like islands in an ocean, she has written the City of Indecisions and Hesitations. His heart trembles, his breath quickens. Here, she has written the words:

"will the same fate happen?......

Maybe.

Maybe not...."

He is frantic now. He is confused. He has no knowledge of what this means. Is this the book he has been looking for? If not, what is it, what is in this book? Is there a future written into it? A prophecy? A past? Why did the room of books show him the Book of the Winds? Why not this book? These are all questions among questions. But what he looks for lies beyond these questions.

Then, it is in his hands.

It is the last book he lifts, and it tears his heart open.

In it lies not a description of the winds, not a catalogue of their names, not where they come from. In it lies not stories, tales, fictions. In this book lies what the winds say.

But the pages are empty. He turns each one to find nothing.

Maybe this is the wrong book. He cannot be sure. He closes the book to examine the cover. It is the second book of winds shown in the Atlas, in the room of books. It is the East wind. It says no thing. He searches again, he knows now there is more than one book of winds. He hears a sigh, he sees the colours of the sun. And the Book of the South wind is before him, it is in his hands. He cannot contain himself, he pulls the book open. This time something is heard. A softness, a whisper.

He can hear that something is said but he cannot quite catch it, cannot quite understand the sounds, cannot catch hold of the words. The words are like the winds. They come and then they are gone. His breath quickens. He closes the book once again. He opens it. Once again a sigh. Once again a soft sound. Once again words he cannot catch hold of. He tries a third time. Whereas the book of the East Wind said no thing, the book of the South Wind tells him what he cannot understand. What are the winds bound to say anyway? He throws the book down. He searches frantically. There must be more books. There must be a book of the West wind, of the North wind. And suddenly, they are there, before him. He looks at them, he hesitates. He needs to know what is written in these books, and yet he is afraid to know. But he remembers the City of Hesitationand Doubt and he immediately tires of his indecision.

He lifts the book of the West Wind first.

The West wind, the lover of Flora, the gentle god.On the cover are the colours of autumn, on the covers are the colours of words of green and red and blue and yellow. But amongst these colours the wind is dressed in black. An island in a sea of colour, an island far to the west. And his heart sinks. Inside are pages with nothing written. Pages with words that can no longer be said. Pages that give the impression of words. But there is nothing there. He does not wait. He lays down the book from his hand and lifts the last book, which was the first book.

It is the Book of the North Wind. And he opens it with trepidation.

It is a torn book, a book with only remnants of pages.A book that when opened lets fly all its small torn pieces into the air to be blown about by the winds.The strips that are left behind cling to the spine of the book and say nothing. But the fragments fly.

The fragments fly.

Each fragment has a mark upon it. Yes, he can see, there is writing on these torn leaves, something is said. Yet the wind blows them and he cannot grasp them in their frantic dance. But he will not cease, he has travelled an atlas of cities and islands and valleys and roads unknown to reach this moment. No, he will not cease. And so he lets himself go into the flow of the north wind the way the fragments dance, and when he falls into their rhythm, they come to him, these words borne by the winds, these words the winds say. And on each piece he captures are written the same words, and it makes his breath quicken and his heart beat.On each fragment is written only one line:

"Whom you love is in your heart..."

The Written Breath of the Other
Translations of the Laxian songs

Part of their hearts

...That is why they do not cease in the translations of Loxian scripts, which they cannot stop themselves from describing. They are convinced that the True Song of the Loxians was written in a time long ago by one of their own, by a Valley-dweller...

They are part of their hearts, the Songs of the Loxians. It is part of their hearts to write and keep writing. And nothing is more written about than the Songs of the Loxians.

Here follows extracts from the Book of Above, some of the writings of the Valley-dwellers which deal with translations and adaptations of three of their most ancient songs.

The first writing of each song gives the Loxian script, which is written under Ea, the river, the third season, the script of the written water shapes. The second writing gives the phonetic of the Loxian language. The last writing gives the most literal translation.

In the song "Water shows the hidden heart" the version given is a truer sense of the names of the various cities and islands and valleys. You will see that the City of Constellations is known to those on the island as the City of the Stillness of Nightshapes, the City of Solitudes has been adapted from the City of Aloneness in the Day, the Room of the Written Breath of the Other has been presented as the Room of Books.

In the songs "Less than a pearl" and "The River sings" the full translations have been given, rather than the adapted version given in The Firstwords.

...In the Book of Above the Valley-dwellers write of love, write of all they love, write of all, of everything. They write of what they know and of what they don't know. They write with their hearts pouring out. Thousands describe autumn. There are poems on each Season. And they write what is not even their own, because it stirs within them a feeling they cannot let go of. They write the Song of the Loxians in many different ways, in many different words, with every ounce of longing in their souls...

Water shows the hidden heart

syoombrraaya

o errusay errheemo may nay
oroommay:
mmer mma o say la na orro
mma a pirrro say a nna
mmer mma o ahe rhay o ymm-b-ear-aya-ah

chrhay nethee prma na so la
a rhea no o eron beo so bay hey
raa deekan ebnsia abrra mma rhay na
ahe rhay o rhay mrhee moay

so pluu vy a vay la
a rhay errusay nethee la rhay na
o rheea no beas t'ear rhee ay na
ahe rhay

chbeea korrheeay a mmay he
errusay syfy raa mayna
errusay mmer koul ahrhaya
ahe rhay o rhay mrhee moay

in ch so a llow
errusay merra a rro yo ho
ymm-b-ear-a-aya-ah
prma na o yo ho
sa pur na o mmay
in byr aya lee merra a rro
in ch so a llow
ymm-b-ear-aya-ah
p-llay muna munana
in ch so a llow
so muor a nay ha

errusay nethee chear o nno ah mmay o
a boor ah mmor rhee ay

chbeea airr ranommayo o llow
so errusay prrhayso amee
rheea errusay chbeea espea rro a nno
ahe rhay

in ju lee aya
so a llow la bay ah
nethee ka na mmor a nno nethee ay
chbea a kaleean o no errusay kanay
ahe rhay o rhay mrhee moay

dh rhay mma llay
sa dh ka llay
da rhay da bay say
ymm syfyoonay
nno mmaydaynay
say ee a rhay moay?

ch t-ear kan essata so mmay o
sy oom brraaya
dy a dy a blay a llow
Ahe rhay

sy syfy aru la mmaya nay
o ymm-b-ear-a-aya-ah
a chvla orrranto orro
beea berus say a mma
ahe rhay o rhay mrhee moay

ymm thay aya a yoho sy

Water shows the hidden heart

in this city of the stillness of night shapes
are the words of the timeplace of the end-other
which speak of a place where the clouds of the sky are weeping,
which tells of the journey of a man with sadness in his heart

he journeys through the city of the thinking that does not end
through time
and beyond the island of the house the colour of the waves
themselves, as it is,
past the straight earth of the journey's end and all that is
found there
he journeys on to find his love

through the valley of is-and-was time
the journey to the city of time ending and not ending
and beyond the isle of those who do not know the end
he journeys on

he comes to the city of the shape of aloneness in the day,
the city of the unknown shape of the end
the city of green and the journey of colours
his is a journey of journeys

the road takes him through
to the city where the sky is dreaming,
this one-who-is-looking-for-whom-he-loves,
where the thinking that does not end is within him.
then come the shape of dreams
and the way of the scent of love lies sky dreaming.
the road takes him,
the one-who-is-looking-for-whom-he-loves
and sings of places that exist not existing.
through silence and through night

the road takes him
to the city that looks at finding the shape of the lost.
it is here one finds everywhere the way.

he comes to the mountain of the shape of the breath
and through the city of the always happening.
beyond this city he comes to the river-tree of where the lost are.
he journeys on

to where the snow lies beside love
and through a road the time of darkness finds,
to the islands that are not anywhere,
he comes to the shore of the island of the city of silver.
the journeys of his love breathes in silence

yet that which the journey may sing
that which the world sings
is a long journey, far, to the place of darkness
of one knowing the night,
the lost shapes of far night.
is this a place ending the journey of love?

he is one of those looking
at the moon through the shape of the trees
heart water hidden love
straight and far and the midnight and the road
he journeys on

his heart hears the parable of the timeshape of night,
the one-who-is-looking-for-whom-he-loves,
and he goes to the room of the written breath of the other.
come the winds to the place and say

whom you love is in your heart

Less than a pearl

Heah viiya

Da rhaysy o`
Mal llayrhee o`
Savayly o`
Kadayly o`

Hey o nay Korrheeay
Ah hey o nay ka ru mmay
Eh hymm a vlla rheea kan
Eh hymm a ka lla mmay o an
O ay ka nee hymm nno hymm
O ay ka nee hymm nno hymm a rhay

Hiiyha*...
Hiiyha...
Hiiyha...
Hiiyha...

Heah viiya mene mmay
A he ah luua no eetay
Eh o thaya rhee lloo ka
Eh o merra man a saa
Hey nal oroommay hymm nno hymm
Ah hey nal bana hymm nno hymm a rhay

Hiiyha...
Hiiyha...
Hiiyha...
Hiiyha...

llaymmayona

Less than a pearl

Long journey to knowledge
Now sings the way
of what was
The world moves

As it is, out of night, the written end of night,
and, as it is, out of night a small-world-shape.
Our words we send beyond the moon
Our words and the shape of world-time
Out of the world to find an answer to our lost words
Out of the world to find an answer in the journey of
the lost word.

We call out into the distance
We call out into the distance

Less than a pearl in the shape of stars
and alone in the shadows our island is unfound
Our endeavours leave the way of the world
Yet our dreams have hope
As it is, nothing written is a lost word
and, as it is, our words may journey to no-one.

We call out into the distance.
We call out into the distance.

Repeat

The River Sings

Ea hymm llayhey

Mmerhymm a rheea kan
Mmerhymm a vlla luua
Ea hymm llay hey
a rhee o mmay
hOroommay o nay rhay
hOroommay he errheemo
h'erraKan sy ay
a rhee a mmay

h'unnin in la go dee rhee?
h'unnin in la go chwk a too?

h'airr rin a kan ahera
h'airr rin a kan orhayna?
Ea nno llow rro;
a rhee a mmay?

h'unnin in la go dee rhee?
h'unnin in la go chwk a too?

Tana mmoree va rhay?
Tana mmor rro nna oom a?
yllea toreeay
a rhee a kan
Korrheeay koda nay a
Korrheeay aru hilla
Vee a kyi a hey
a rhee a mmay

Yll yyka pirr o bay ru
Ylyka kalla kwyay la
Ona hanee ay
a rhee o mmay?

h'unnin in la go dee rhee?
h'unnin in la go chwk a too?

Mmerhymm a rheea kan
Mmerhymm a vlla luua
Ea hymm llay hey
a rhee o mmay

hOroommay o nay rhay
hOroommay he errheemo
h'erraKan sy ay
a rhee a mmay

h'airr rin a kan ahera
h'airr rin a kan orhayna?
Ea nno llow rro;
a rhee a mmay?

h'unnin in la go dee rhee?
h'unnin in la go chwk a too?

Tana mmoree va rhay?
Tana mmor rro nna oom a?
Yllea toreeay
a rhee a kan
Korrheeay koda nay a
Korrheeay aru hilla
Vee a kyi a hey
a rhee a mmay
Yll yyka pirr o bay ru
Ylyka kalla kwyay la
Ona hanee ay
a rhee o mmay?

A rhee o mmay…

The river sings

Our words go beyond the moon.
Our words go into the shadows.
The river sings out the words
of the shape of the endlessness.
We write of our journey through night.
We write in our aloneness in the stillness.
The erraKan* want to know the shape of eternity.

Who knows the way it is?
Who knows why time will not tell us?

We have the mountains, the moon and solitude.
Will they be with us to the journey's end?
The river holds the lost road of the sky;
the shape of eternity?

Who knows the way it is?
Who knows why time will not tell us?

Where is the beginning, where is the end?
When did the sky first cry tears?
The erraEa* asks
is the end found in the endlessness?
Day and night are in the unknown.
The day tells us the measure of time.
Why are we calling out into the endlessness?

One's world is the colour of a small cloud.
We are but a moment in time.
What is the answer that is found in the endlessness?

Who knows the way it is?
Who knows why time will not tell us?

Our words go beyond the moon.
Our words go into the shadows.
The river sings out the words
of the shape of the endlessness.
We write of our journey through night.
We write in our aloneness in the stillness.
The erraKan* want to know the shape of eternity.

We have the mountains, the moon and solitude.
Will they be with us to the journey's end?
The river holds the lost road of the sky;
the shape of eternity?

Who knows the way it is?
Who knows why time will not tell us?

Where is the beginning, where is the end?
When did the sky first cry tears?
The erraEa* asks
is the end found in the endlessness?
Day and night are in the unknown.
The day tells us the measure of time.
Why are we calling out into the endlessness?
One's world is the colour of a small cloud.
We are but a moment in time.
What is the answer that is found in the endlessness?

The endlessness...

---

* erraKan - the Loxians, the people with the moon as their emblem.
* erraEa – the River people, Valley-dwellers. The river is their emblem
* yllea – a River person, a Riparian.

This line comes from one of the early writings found in the Black Book of the Night.

The writing is as follows:

zay b'ayor zay b'ayor ay ashna rro maa?

zay b'ayor zay b'ayor ay a's nna rro mma?
zay b'ayor zayb'ayor a sna rro mma?
zay b'ayor zay b'ayor ay ashna rro mma?

zay b'ayor zay b'ayor a's nna rro mma?
zay b'ayor zay b'ayor ay a sna rro mma?
zay b'ayor zay b'ayor ay ashna rro mma?

zay b'ayor zay b'ayor ah s nna rro mma?
zay b'ayor zay b'ayor ay a sna rro mma?
zay b'ayor zay b'ayor ay ashna rro mma?

zay b'ayor zay b'ayor ah s nna rro mma?
zay b'ayor zay b'ayor ay a sna rro maa?
zay b'ayor zayb'ayor ay a's na rro maa?

zay b'ayor zay b'ayor ay ashna rro mma?
zay b'ayor zay b'ayor ay ashna rro maa...
zay b'ayor zay b'ayor ay ashna rro maa...

Neverending

The love who writes love
-and does the sky speak love in words of tears?
-is what the sky says lost?
-does the neverending sky say love?

The love who writes love
-is the sky speaking through tears?
-is the love the sky says lost?
-does the sky speak of the neverending?

The love who writes love
-is the beginning the sky crying?
-who finds what the lost sky says?
-is love found in the neverending?

The love who writes love
-who knows what the words the sky lost say?
-is all love lost and found in the sky?
-will the sky find the lost love?

The love who writes love
is love neverending?
love neverending…
neverending…

Glossary

Let me tell you...

Immrama - In Celtic Mythology great sea voyages which take one to other worldly islands.

Purrhayso - in Loxian language it is a "through-a-dream-journey". This is a term used for emotional experiences visualised as a journey.

Odyssesy - Homer's epic poem in which the Odyssey represents a long series of wanderings. Also used to describe a long process of change.

of words that exist...

Name of season	Season	Alphabet
Essa (leaves)	autumn	orBerummay (written wind shape)
Ju (snow/north)	winter	orJummay (written snow shapes)
Ea (river)	third	orOommmay (written water shapes)
Pirrro (rain)	spring	orPirrrommay (written sky-crying shapes)
Luua (shadow)	summer	orLuuammay (written shadow shapes)
Kan (moon)	sixth	orKanmmay (written moon shapes)

The Room of Books

zay b'ayor zay b'ayor - an expression of love. It literally means 'the love who writes love' It uses one of the "uniques" - the letter z. It is the only time the letter z is used in the loxian scripts. The expression is taken from one of the early writings in The Black Book of the Night. An excerpt of this writing is given in The Written Breath of the Other - the Translations.

less than a pearl

hiiyha - from the word heyiilllaymayna – as it is, we sing distance

The river sings

llaymmayona - sing the shape to/of the end - repeat
laola - time to/of time - can also be used for repeat